Virgin at Sonoma

BARBIE O'CONNOR

All Rights Reserved
Published in the United States
by Zunné Group Racing, Inc.
Racing Resort Ranch is a registered trademark of
Zunne Group Racing, Inc.
Library of Congress Cataloging-in-Publication Data
O'Connor, Barbie
Virgin at the Speedway/Barbie O'Connor
ISBN 10: 0-997-5767-2-3
ISBN 13: 978-0-9975767-2-6
eBook ISBN 13: 978-0-9975767-3-3
Cover design by Eli Miller

For Buddy

You were always there for me as I made my way through the writing process

At my feet and by my side

Ready for a walk at any time

Someone to talk to when I didn't know which way to go

Your unconditional love touched me

I miss you

PROLOGUE

Working quickly, he plunged the syringe up to its hilt into the vial. He drew the plunger back to pull clear liquid into the barrel, careful to avoid any air bubbles. Capping the needle, he taped the syringe open, wrapped the package in soft cloth, slid it into a maroon calfskin leather cigar case, and placed that case in the inside pocket of his jacket. Now all he needed was the right opportunity to push the plunger home. At that point he could take control of Chateau La Mer.

He remembered the stories told to him about World War II and the espionage afterward. Members of the Resistance still hunted their enemies, killing them subtly, leaving little trace besides the unusual symptoms their victims suffered. His father's death had left him with a desire for revenge, and he hoped that burning goal was coming to fruition, for he now knew his father's nemesis was at Chateau La Mer.

He wanted to wipe these men out, just as his family was

wiped out in Germany and afterward in France when the war was over. He'd learned many talents from his grandfather, who stayed away from the front lines because he was a magician with pen and ink, able to create such realistic counterfeit cash that they never lacked for anything and were held in high regard by the government in power.

In the last days of the war, when anyone with half a brain knew who was going to win and who was going to lose, his family, posing as refugees from Belgium, presented beautifully forged identity documents and traveled to France. They settled in a small village: they took over a cottage and blended in with the locals, who at first accepted them as the cousins of Madame Tatin.

They opened a small café and listened carefully to all the conversations as they served the patrons at their tables. It was there that his father one night drank a little too much wine and shared the family secret of what Grandfather did in the war and how the family, whose German accents rolled into their French conversation, had survived.

The next night, after a few bottles of the local red wine from Chateau Bernard were delivered as a gift, the family closed the café for the night and cooked a special meal to celebrate their new life in France, in a village that had now signaled its welcome.

The father, who had organized the party, wanted everyone in the family to attend. Yet when he saw his boy, not yet three years old, deep in slumber, he let him be. And when he urged Grandfather to join in the fun, the old man begged off, coughing and wheezing from a bad cold, wanting to sleep. While the rest of the family savored the wine and food in celebration of their acceptance in the small village, the old man dozed in bed, happily listening to their songs and merry talk.

That night, after they had drunk all the wine and eaten all the food, most of the family suffered symptoms similar to dysentery. Almost all of them died: only the grandfather and the young boy survived.

CHAPTER 1

Looking around at the carefully set table, with its pristine white linen tablecloth and napkins, shimmering crystal goblets, and glimmering silver flatware, Luz Maria Dane, family investment adviser to the Slattery clan, read the place cards at the head table for the Chateau La Mer wine dinner benefiting the San Antonio Children's Home. She was seated between Orval Slattery, the chairman of the board of Chateau La Mer, and Jeff Harwood, her friend and lover. Other guests at the table were Sara Slattery, Orval's granddaughter; Julienne Cohen, the owner of the liquor distribution company cosponsoring the dinner; her husband, Martin Cohen, Orval's estate planning attorney; Sacha Bernard, Orval's partner and friend, who along with winemaker Paul Angel founded Chateau La Mer in the early 1980s; and Clint and Michelle Amberson, who were Sara's aunt and uncle and also Jeff's partners in Amberson-Harwood Racing. It promised to be a fabulous evening for oenophiles, with a blind tasting of a selection of French wines to compare to the Chateau La Mer creations.

During the cocktail hour, when champagne was served with canapés, Luz, in a stunning midnight-blue strapless dress sprinkled with iridescent sequins, made the rounds to meet and greet friends and clients. On her return to Emerson York after her work at the Indy 500, her manager had met all of her new ideas for prospecting new clients or educating old ones with stony resistance. He was jealous of her ability to multitask while at the track, where she worked with her clients via phone, text, and email in the morning and then in the afternoon focused her efforts on getting the car qualified and ready to race. His inflexibility led her to make the difficult decision to leave Emerson York and start her own investment advisory firm, L. M. Dane, LLC. She'd been told that she'd never be able to make it, that her clients would not move from the big New York firm, but the mortgage crisis and the unforeseen failure of so many Wall Street firms had given her the advantage when she started off on her own.

Now her everyday world was one of evaluating portfolios, rebalancing asset allocations, proposing new investment choices, and listening to the needs of her clients. Luz and Jeff had worked side by side only a few months before, in May, running their open-wheel race team at the Indy 500. She missed all the elements of being at the track: the people who worked on the teams, the sounds of the engines, the chess-like strategy required to qualify and win, and the frenzy of getting everything ready in very little time and fixing last-minute problems. Luz thrilled at the sensation of thirty-three high-performance engines starting simultaneously and then forming a synchronized, balletic train as the starting grid of cars shrieked up to speed at the start of the race. It was the rush of a lifetime: she could still recall the distinctive smell of race fuel when the engines started and feel the wind as it whipped by her when the cars barreled down the front straightaway.

By starting a new life for herself with her own firm and the clients she loved, she hoped to combine the best elements of the two worlds she knew. Seeing Clint and Michelle again brought it all back to her. Luz wanted that balance, that love, that excitement, that fulfillment in her own life too.

When the bell sounded for dinner, Luz looked around the crowd to find Jeff, who was immersed in conversation with a local banker. Dressed in a tuxedo and wearing his race car–motif bow tie and cummerbund, he cut a handsome figure in the crowd, and she was delighted to see him so animated as he talked with the banker in front of him. Still, it was time. She slowly walked toward him, catching his eye and making the wind-it-up signal with her index finger to get him to wrap up his chat.

"Hello, handsome," Luz said as she leaned in to kiss Jeff's cheek, and then said to the banker, "Great to see you, Greg. What has Jeff been bending your ear about? Something interesting, I hope."

Greg exchanged a look with Jeff, and a secret smile passed between them.

"He's just letting me know some ideas he has for the future. Pretty interesting ideas, I do say. But he asked me to keep it private for now, so I'll honor his request for the time being."

"Oh, good! I like secrets," Luz said, her sparkling blue eyes intent on Jeff's green ones. "Maybe someday he'll share those with me."

"You know I'll tell you all about it when the time is right, but not yet, not yet." Jeff took her arm, patted her hand, and led her forward into the ballroom.

Once they were seated, Julienne Cohen rose to the podium to welcome the guests. She shared the mission statement of the Children's Home and thanked Chateau La Mer for their contribution to the event. In appreciation she invited Orval Slattery and Sacha Bernard to the podium and presented them with hand-blown glass wine globes made by a local artist to commemorate the evening. With a thick head of silver-gray hair, aquamarine eyes, and a light tan, Orval, who was about six feet tall, fit and trim, climbed the stairs to the stage unassisted and sauntered to the podium, where he greeted Julienne with the double cheek kiss so popular in Europe.

Sacha lumbered behind him, his stocky slightly taller frame, gave the impression he was a friendly bear, with full longish dark hair and a brushy but exquisitely trimmed mustache. His golden-brown eyes twinkled with delight as he hugged Julienne and planted two wet kisses on her cheeks.

"Thank you, Julienne," Orval said. "It is always a pleasure to be in San Antonio, especially for an event to support the Children's Home."

"*Oui, mon ami!*" Sacha echoed, "an important cause worthy of our support." He looked at Orval with amusement in his eyes. "Are you ready to share our big news?"

"Certainly, Sacha. There is no time like the present," Orval said. "Please go ahead."

"There has been a great deal of speculation about the future of Chateau La Mer. Orval, Paul, and I envision a long and independent future for our vineyards and winery. We prefer that to being gobbled up by a large conglomerate where we will just be one small bead in a necklace of assets," Sacha began, and then Orval took over.

"I'm quite lucky this evening to be accompanied by my granddaughter, Sara Slattery. Many of you know her, since she grew up here in the Alamo City. After she graduates from Texas A&M this spring with a specialization in viticulture and oenology, Sara will be coming aboard Chateau La Mer!"

The crowd murmured excitedly, then broke into applause. There had been much speculation about who would succeed in the leadership role at the famous winery. The wine critics who'd arrived from all over the country busily made note of this announcement, which would rock the wine world. Paparazzi captured the event for their publications, and the local news media was filming the announcement: they knew it would ultimately be broadcast on most of the food entertainment channels around the globe.

As he stood beaming and smiling, basking in the happy moment, he motioned for his partner, Sacha Bernard, to pour them both a glass of wine. Sacha grasped the bottle of Chateau La Mer cabernet sauvignon and poured about two inches into each of the hand-blown glasses recently presented to them. He handed one to Sacha, then swirled the wine in the glass, holding it up to the overhead light. "Nice legs, eh?"

His jovial reference to one of the attributes of a fine wine—

the glycerin in the wine as it slides down the glass creates the illusion of a chorus line of attractive feminine legs—got laughs from the many wine connoisseurs in the room. Critically eyeing the wine they were noted for, Sacha chuckled, stroking his mustache.

All eyes were on Orval as he inhaled the bouquet with a practiced manner befitting a renowned winemaker. Then he raised his glass.

"To my granddaughter, Sara. May she enjoy the fruits of her labor by creating a wine to rival any of the premier cru vintages of France. À *votre santé!*"

He and Sacha toasted Sara with the presentation glasses. A cheerful repetition of the familiar French toast echoed around the room. Photographers eager for the perfect shot of Orval Slattery and Sacha Bernard crowded nearby. Just as Sacha and Orval touched glasses, one of the photographers bumped Sacha, causing him to lose his grip on his glass. It fell to the floor and shattered.

"Would someone get him another glass, please?" Orval said to the room.

Luz quickly grabbed the full glass at Sacha's place from their table and handed it to him.

"You always were a clumsy one, Sacha," Orval teased. "All the wine we've spilled over time would probably fill every glass in this room!"

Everyone laughed, and he continued, "To our friendship, and partnership, and to my granddaughter, Sara."

Orval drank fully from his glass, as did Sacha. Sara glanced around at the others at her table, unsure what to do, as she considered it bad luck to drink a toast to herself. Then, smoothing the skirt of her red silk taffeta dress, she nervously pushed her auburn hair away from her face and smiled as she surveyed the crowd in the candlelit ballroom. Looking up at the glowing face of her ninety-year-old grandfather and his partner, she raised her glass to both of them, grateful for their faith in her as a future leader of the world-famous winery. Both men winked at her, waving their glasses in her direction.

Orval encouraged everyone to make their best guess during the dinner and blind tasting about which wines they were enjoying, and which ones they thought were the best.

"Chateau La Mer, of course! Although Sacha has also strategically brought in a few bottles of the award-winning Chateau Bernard for your tasting pleasure!" Orval tossed out that remark with a generous smile at his barrel-chested partner.

With that encouragement the short program was over. Holding on to the short railing, Slattery made his way down the three stairs from the stage and then to his chair at the head table.

As he sat down, he began to totter a bit. Sara was accustomed to this slight balance issue: it was a side effect of the stroke he'd suffered a few years before. Rising from her seat to stabilize him and push him toward the center of his chair, Sara found herself falling as well, her grandfather's body a sudden deadweight that carried the two of them directly onto the lap of Luz Dane, who yelped in surprise at the avalanche of bodies falling on top of her. At first it seemed like an overcorrection, and as Martin Cohen helped Sara to her feet, they assumed Slattery would jauntily laugh at his own clumsiness, his usual response to his teetering ways, and right himself with a little help from a friend. When Jeff Harwood put one arm around the old man's back and with the other took hold of Slattery's left arm, gently pulling him up off Luz's lap, he found the body slack. Carefully Jeff placed him in a chair, touched his neck, looked for an indication of a pulse, and saw that the man's clammy skin was turning a pale gray.

"Someone call a doctor, an ambulance," Jeff said. "I don't think he's feeling well."

Julienne Cohen called 911, leaving her place at the table to notify the front desk that an ambulance had been called and to direct them to the ballroom.

Sacha quickly wet one of the table napkins with cold water and placed it across Orval's forehead, then stood and looked around the room, feeling stunned. The episode had frightened him, bringing back memories from his childhood.

During World War II, they had lived out the Nazi occupation of France by working in the grape vineyards of Chateau Bernard, which belonged to Sacha's family. Sacha had been only ten years old when he found Orval, an American soldier who had been wounded and was barely alive, hidden among the vines in the family vineyard. Sacha and Paul Angel—his boyhood friend and their other partner in Chateau La Mer—hid Orval in plain sight, posing him as an illiterate vineyard worker in rags in the fields once he was healthy again. Seeing his friend in this weakened state reminded him of the terrors of the past.

At other tables the guests were eating salad and bread, sipping the wine, discussing how the flavors married with the two wines poured to go with the appetizer, oblivious to the chaos at the head table, which was located at the front of the ballroom rather than the center.

Michelle, following Sacha's lead, dipped her napkin in ice water and wrapped it around the back of Slattery's neck. Clint hobbled out the nearest door so he could direct the emergency medical technicians to the most convenient ballroom entrance and table. Martin, Luz, and Jeff put their chairs together to create a makeshift cot they could lay the old man down on, since he kept falling forward when he was seated. Slattery, still unconscious, kept murmuring under his breath. Sara stood nearby wringing her napkin, her face pale as moonlight.

Within minutes the sound of a siren was heard outside the hotel, and Clint, pointing with his cane, led a team of emergency medical technicians bearing a stretcher through the ballroom doorway and directed them to the table where Orval Slattery lay. Quickly they loaded him onto the gurney and took him outside, where they verified his thready pulse, placed an oxygen mask over his mouth and nose, and checked other vital signs as they moved toward the ambulance.

Michelle, Clint, Sacha, Luz, and Jeff followed along, bringing a stunned Sara with them. Before they left the party, they hurriedly said their goodbyes to Julienne and Martin, promising to keep them apprised of Orval's situation.

Once Orval was entrusted to the medical personnel, Julienne and Martin Cohen moved through the ballroom, going from one table to the next to inform the guests of the situation and assure them that everything was being done for Mr. Slattery. They reminded them that Orval wanted them to have a wonderful evening enjoying a great meal and his outstanding wine.

Jeff drove Luz, Sara, Clint, and Michelle to the hospital in the SUV, while Sacha followed along in his own car. Luz rode shotgun, and Clint and Michelle sat in the back seat with Sara between them. Michelle had her arm around the younger woman, holding her close

Once they were on their way, Sara spoke up, her voice hesitant. "I didn't know he was so vulnerable. We just spent the weekend at a friend's ranch and he seemed fine. I don't know what happened. Except for the stroke a few years ago, he's been doing everything right. Vitamins, healthy diet, exercise. I just don't understand."

Clint turned to Sara. "Honey, I thought I was doing everything right, and look where that got me. That stroke really set me back, but sometimes things happen to our bodies to make us examine our lives, to get us straight in our heads. These little events are God's way of getting our attention. It may be time for your grandfather to retire. Maybe he's been holding on to the reins a little too tight."

Once they pulled up behind the ambulance at the emergency room, Luz and Sara walked to the check-in desk. Sara was instructed to follow the gurney into the triage area, while Luz took care of the administrative issues as best she could. Most of the information she already knew from her dealings with Orval regarding his personal investments and assisting him with his estate planning. By the time she was through with the paperwork, which only lacked Sara's signature as his next-of-kin, Clint, Michelle, Sacha, and Jeff were all seated in the adjacent alcove awaiting news from the doctors.

While they waited they perused the year-old magazines littering the tables and chairs in the waiting room. Shortly afterward, Sara came back out to the waiting area, her eyes red from crying, her cheeks streaked with tears.

Michelle and Luz rushed to her. Michelle hugged her and dabbed at the tears on her face with tissues, while Luz took her handbag from her.

"Don't worry, Sara. He'll be fine. I bet he forgot to eat lunch and his blood sugar was low," Michelle said.

The three women sat down. Sara nervously smoothed her dress, and Luz patted her arm. Michelle smiled at both of them. Obviously anxious, Sara stood up abruptly and announced she was going to the ladies' room. She grabbed her purse from Luz and as she did it fell open spilling its contents all over the waiting room floor. Luz bent down to help pick things up, handing them to Sara as she did. Sara quickly rushed away, tears rolling down her cheeks.

After she sat down again, Luz noticed a small silver cylinder that was under a table across the room. Figuring it was a perfume atomizer that belonged to Sara, she knelt down to get it so she could return it to her. Out of curiosity she uncapped it and smelled the contents which reeked of a mixture of alcohol and almonds. Then she put it into the pocket of her dress.

About twenty minutes later, one of the doctors came out to the waiting room and approached their small group. "I take it from how y'all are dressed that you must have been attending some sort of gala. I have a few questions and wondered if we could talk in a more private area."

Clint looked at Michelle, while Luz and Jeff caught each other's eye. Clint was the first to speak. "Sure. We'd be happy to oblige."

The doctor led the six of them to a small conference room, and they sat down at the table.

"Since Mr. Slattery fell ill at a public event, we want to gather information about what everyone remembers while it is fresh," the doctor said. "He is probably going to be just fine, but we noticed some signs that caused us to think that maybe there was something he ate or drank that caused his collapse."

At that moment, the door to the small room opened, and in walked a tall, dark-haired, rail-thin man who introduced himself as Detective Travis Boone of the local police department.

Holding the door open, tilting his head toward the hallway, he said, "I'll take it from here, Doc."

The doctor nodded, then exited the room, after saying goodbye to the group.

Detective Boone looked around the table. "We just want you to tell us what you remember, and then tomorrow when Mr. Slattery is better, all this won't matter."

Opening a spiral notebook, the detective smoothed the page, put his pen to paper, and asked, "How is it that you are all together? Is this the night of the Children's Home wine dinner gala?" He added, "I got an invitation, but with my schedule, it's hard to go to one of those shindigs."

Michelle spoke up in her most assertive fashion,

"Yes, Mr. Slattery was the guest presenter at the event. His winery provided all the wine for the dinner. He is originally from San Antonio, and lives half the time here and the other half in the Napa Valley near his vineyards. Sara is his grand-daughter, as well as my niece. Her mother was my sister. Her father was Orval Slattery's son. Unfortunately, both of them died young. My sister died from breast cancer three years ago. Her father lost his life in a boating accident off the Pacific coast last year. Sara's had a rough couple of years."

"And you three," the detective asked, gesturing toward Sacha, Luz, and Jeff, "what about you?"

Sacha spoke up first. "Orval is my partner, along with Paul Angel, our winemaker, in Chateau La Mer. We made a very important announcement tonight. It will make a big difference in the wine business and in the value of the winery."

That piqued the detective's curiosity. "What was the announcement?"

"Sara, his granddaughter, will take his place in management at the winery," Sacha answered. "She is now studying oenology and viticulture, and she has also interned at the winery for the last eight summers, since she was fourteen years old. Orval told me his plans many years ago for giving her a portion of his partnership interest every year, as part of his estate plan."

He looked over at Luz for confirmation of what he shared with the detective about Orval and his plans for his interest in Chateau La Mer.

Luz nodded. "I'm Mr. Slattery's investment advisor and financial planner. I can't discuss the details, but I can tell you that over the last few days I've been in meetings with Mr. Slattery and his attorney, Martin Cohen, to review his financial plans."

She waited while the detective made notes.

Clint said, "This young man is Jeff Harwood, my partner in Amberson-Harwood Racing. If it weren't for him and Ms. Dane, my team would not have won the Indy 500."

The detective nodded, listening intently and making a few more notes. At that moment another doctor, this one a man about Clint's age, walked into the small conference room. He introduced himself as an old friend of Orval Slattery's, and after he shook everyone's hand, then asked, "Detective Boone, you don't mind if I ask a few questions of my own, do you? When I heard Orval was here, I came right down."

Boone nodded his assent, and the grizzled doctor, his hands clasped in front of him asked, "So what really happened tonight?"

All of the group members shared what they recalled about the presentation and toast. Sacha demonstrated the red wine stain on his tuxedo shirt—the result of the photographer getting a little too close and causing him to drop his glass.

"How did the wine get to the dinner?" asked the older doctor in a casual tone.

Sacha answered, "When he appears personally at a dinner, Orval brings the cases of wine with him on his private plane to the city where the event takes place. He also brings a couple of magnum-size bottles in a thermal carry-on that he provides to the head table, and for use on the podium when he speaks and makes a toast."

"Why are they packaged separately?"

"Magnums are double the size of regular bottles, so it's easier to see the labels from far away. It is his signature statement at an event. He and Paul Angel have been doing it this way ever since I can remember," Sacha explained.

The two men nodded and looked at each other, then the older one spoke. "We've kept you long enough. We have all your contact information; in case we have any other questions. Hopefully Mr. Slattery will feel better tomorrow."

Clint led the way out, hobbling to the parking lot with Jeff and Sacha by his side. Luz lagged behind the group, debating about what to do with the silver cylinder she found in the waiting room. Not believing Sara would poison her elderly grandfather to gain her inheritance early, Luz knew that she had to share any evidence she had with the police detective.

"Detective Boone, I...I have something to give you," Luz said in a soft voice.

She held out the silver cylinder she'd extracted from her pocket and said, "Earlier, I found this on the floor in the waiting room. It was after everything in Sara's purse spilled out of it. It is a perfume atomizer. It smells very much like almonds."

With his handkerchief, he wrapped it up and placed it in an evidence bag he had with him. "We'll check it for fingerprints and see what else we can learn from it."

"But, mine are on it. I just picked it up," Luz said, worriedly.

"It was wise of you to give it to me now. For your sake, I hope there are some other prints here, or you may be a suspect, too," he said, sternly.

"Yes, I understand," Luz said gravely, her face drawn, "Goodnight, Detective Boone," she said as she turned and walked to the door.

"Goodbye, Ms. Dane. Thank you for your cooperation," the

detective said, icily, as she walked out the door of the building.

Luz quickly walked to the parking lot where the Ambersons, Jeff, Sara and Sacha all waited for her.

"What kept you so long?" Jeff asked impatiently.

"I...I had to go to the ladies' room. Sorry, I held everyone up," Luz said, hoping she would not regret her decision to hand over the perfume case.

They boarded the SUV and brought it around to the emergency room entrance. Again, Sacha followed them in his rental car.

"Since we are halfway home anyway, and Sacha and Sara are staying with us, why don't we ride with him?" Michelle said. "You can take our SUV and we'll figure it all out tomorrow. Let's meet back here in the morning around ten o'clock to check in on Orval and then we can get Sacha to the airport. OK with everyone?"

Sacha gallantly opened the back doors of the Mercedes sedan he'd rented, and helped the ladies in. Clint settled carefully in the front seat and waved goodbye as they drove out of the parking lot. Luz and Jeff looked at one another shyly. They'd been apart for the three months since Indy, with Luz starting her own business and Jeff running the team from one track to another across the United States.

"Are you hungry?" Jeff asked as they walked to the car.

"Yes, I'm starving. All I had was one appetizer and a glass of champagne," she answered, and then grinned. "Fat bomb?"

"Hell, yes," Jeff said, as he fired up the SUV, and headed toward their favorite fast hamburger joint, where he always got a double cheeseburger and she ordered a special with jalapeno-jack cheese and sliced peppers and onions on top.

Walking under the orange-and-white-striped awning into the all-night restaurant, Jeff and Luz, in their tux and ball gown, caused a stir among the other patrons, most of whom were in their pajama bottoms and T-shirts. At that point Jeff realized they might be more comfortable eating at home, so he ordered their meals to go. Luz insisted they go to her condo, since it was close by.

BARBIE O'CONNOR

CHAPTER 2

They walked into her condo, the lights of the city twinkling through the balcony doors. Jeff handed her the paper sack of hot food. "Let's put this in the microwave to stay warm for a little while. Please excuse me, OK?" He headed toward the bath and bedroom.

Luz went to the kitchen and placed the bag in the microwave. She took two champagne flutes out of the cupboard and grabbed a bottle of cold bubbly from the fridge. She removed the cork from the bottle so gently that only a soft *pfft* sound escaped from it, then set it in a silver ice bucket filled with ice and water.

Once the ice bucket and glasses were on a tray, cocktail napkins at the ready, Luz moved everything onto the glass coffee table in front of the sofa and poured two glasses.

As she poured the champagne, she heard the beginning of a jazzy version of a Rat Pack–era ballad, a love song she and

Jeff last danced to after the Indy awards banquet just a few months before. He'd started the album on the turntable as he came back into the room.

Sitting down beside her, he handed her one of the flutes with a napkin and took the other for himself.

"To being together again," he said, touching the edge of her glass so lightly that his toast sounded like a soft bell.

He looked carefully at Luz, examining her face, framed by a few curly tendrils of her jet-black hair. She was wearing the chandelier earrings he'd given her, their tiny diamonds sparkling in the candlelight. Her eyes, like midnight-blue pools of water, reflected his face and the pinpoints of light from the city. She wore no necklace, and her skin, like creamy coffee, was smooth against his touch. Jeff stroked her cheek. Her full lips, naked of lipstick, beckoned to him. He kissed her.

"You've been busy," he said. "Too busy to join me at the track."

"Yes, lots of meetings with former clients. Making sure I have all the paperwork in order. It has taken a lot of time. New people have heard I've started my own firm and they've approached me, too," Luz said, looking out at the city lights. "You've had a great year so far. A lot of podium finishes for the team. And Clint and Michelle tell me how you are doing."

"Yeah, we've had a lot of podium finishes," Jeff answered. He paused, then continued. "I thought you'd have more time once you had your own firm, not less. I thought you'd be by my side more these last few months. What happened?"

He poured them each another glass of champagne. As he handed Luz her refilled flute, he saw that her eyes were glistening with tears, so he gave her his handkerchief.

"Honey, what's wrong?"

"Oh, Jeff, it took a lot of work to make that transition. With the mortgage crisis, Emerson York was slow in releasing the accounts. Clients were unsure what to do. I wasn't sure I was going to have enough clients to support my own firm for a few weeks there. It was a mess," she said, sniffling. "And you weren't here, so I just dove headfirst into my work, which was the worst thing I could do, because it consumed me. That was all I did. I am so out of balance right now." Then she brightened up a bit and smiled. "But I'm planning to make it to Sonoma."

"I'm glad to hear that. Let's see if we can help you get back into balance," Jeff said, standing up and offering her his hand. "Care to dance?"

Taking his hand, Luz was soon nestled against his chest, humming along with the music, as he led her through a few simple twirls and turns, with a simple fox-trot step in between. The next song evoked special memories for both of them, so they continued to dance.

"I've missed you," Luz said.

"I have to confess, I've missed you, too. I guess that is why I am a little peeved with you about starting your own firm. I thought we'd have more time together rather than less."

"I think the hardest part is over. Kind of like racing, it's a thrash at the beginning, but then you get into a rhythm and go," Luz said softly, hoping Jeff would understand he was important to her.

Luz nuzzled his ear and took over the dance lead from him, moving the two of them down the hallway to her bedroom.

Surprised to find her room lit by candles, Luz giggled. "You've been busy."

Votive candles, scattered on bedside tables and her dresser, cast a soft flickering light around the room. "Yes, I was thinking along the same lines as you. We both need a little romance," he said. "Let me add a little sparkle to the room."

Jeff brought in the tray with the champagne flutes and ice bucket and placed them on the side table.

Loosely embracing each other, swaying with the music, they looked into one another's eyes. Beginning at her shoulders, he slowly drew his fingers down her bare arms, to the finger tips on her right hand. He tenderly kissed the back of that hand and, starting with her pinky, kissed each finger until he reached her thumb, which he sucked gently before turning her hand over and kissing her palm.

Flushing a rosy-pink from the valley between her breasts, Luz began to breathe deeply as Jeff started on her left hand. She was his willing captive as he held on to both her hands.

After he'd finished with her hands, he twirled her around so that her back was toward him, then he slowly unzipped her dress, allowing it to slide off her into a puddle on the floor.

Carefully stepping sideways to avoid her clothes, he twirled Luz around to face him. Taking her in his arms as if to waltz, he danced her back onto the bed.

Then he let go. "Care for some champagne?"

Luz laughed deeply as her body shuddered.

"I'll take that as a yes," Jeff said, pouring an inch or two in each glass. Then he took a swig from his flute, leaned over Luz, and put his mouth on hers, slowly releasing the champagne bubbles into her mouth.

"Tastes good, doesn't it?" he said as she lay back on the pillows, basking in the moment.

While she watched him, Jeff undid his tux tie, unbuttoned his shirt, and then finished taking off his clothes. Luz reached for him. As they embraced, slowly rocking, moving together as one, they cried out, singing each other's name to the heavens, grateful for the reunion they had been anticipating over the last three months.

Soaked from their sweat, Luz stood up, stumbling as she did so, eyeing Jeff hungrily. "Again?" she asked.

Jeff nodded, trying to sit up. "But I need a little sustenance before I go another round with you, and maybe a glass of ice water and a towel."

Luz sauntered into the kitchen and brought back the requested items. Then she returned to the microwave and warmed up their burgers as Jeff gulped down the ice water. Luz brought the food and they began to eat. Making sure he'd swallowed his first bites, she took a sip of champagne and, closing her mouth on his, let loose the cold, sparkling bubbles as a chaser.

Jeff groaned.

"Burgers and champagne—could I ask for more?" he said, as he watched her, taking in all of her voluptuous flesh, savoring the flavors in his mouth and his memory.

As she walked by the bed, he grabbed her hand and pulled her down next to him. Rolling across the bed, taking turns, they made love all night, one on top of the other, standing and sitting, every position they could muster, only stopping to eat and drink.

At about four in the morning, Jeff sat on the edge of the bed and poured the last of the champagne into their glasses. "We've been going at it at least five hours," he said through his gasps. I mean, it's been three months since we've been together, and I'm a little out of shape."

Luz lay back down on the bed and coyly stroked his back running her fingers from the back of his neck down to his hips. Jeff moaned, and then he rolled over and beckoned her to mount him. With a light, playful slap of his hand across her buttocks, Jeff said, "Ride 'em, cowgirl!" and Luz did. After their excitement and pleasure peaked again, their bodies vibrating as one, they collapsed in each other's arms and fell asleep, spent from their loving reunion.

CHAPTER 3

Awaking as sunlight filled the bedroom, Luz left Jeff snoring softly and went to the kitchen to fix coffee. Hungry and sore from the night before, Luz took a long hot shower, stretching slowly and relishing the water running over her body.

Abruptly the shower curtain was pushed aside, surprising Luz in her reverie. She yelped, "What, what's going on?"

"I thought you'd wait for me, so we could do this together. Or have you forgotten how good it feels to have someone else scrub your back?" Jeff said, armed with a fluffy shower pouf. He stepped into the cascade of water that had filled the room with steam.

Luz turned and put her arms around him and kissed him, full of desire. Jeff gave her just a brief peck on the lips. "What was that? That wasn't a real kiss," she whined.

"We don't have time for anything more than a quick kiss and a good shower. Remember, we're meeting everyone at the hospital at ten o'clock, and we may need some extra time to get dressed. That mark on your neck is not suitable for children to see," Jeff said with a stern look that morphed into a mischievous grin.

Luz clapped her hand over the dark red blotch right at the nape of her neck, where she could still feel Jeff's lips from the night before.

"Oh, my, yes. I was so caught up with you last night that I forgot about...everything," she said.

Jeff kissed her neck lightly as he scrubbed her back, "Good. I'm glad I still have that effect on you. And now that you are all clean and rinsed off, be a good girl and get out of the shower so I can shave and finish my bath."

Luz hopped out of the shower, grabbed her towel, and wiped a circle of the mirror clear of steam so she could examine her hickey wondering how to cover it up. She wandered back to the kitchen, poured coffee in two mugs, toasted the English muffins she'd set out, and brought everything back to the bedroom on a tray.

While she towel-dried her hair, Luz straightened up the room, picking up item after item, beginning with their fancy clothes and moving on to the paper bag full of yellow burger wrappings and cold French fries. She picked up the flutes, champagne bottle, and chiller, smiling at the memory of the night before. Once she got everything tidied up and had a sip of coffee and a bite of muffin with jam and peanut butter, Luz started to feel she could handle whatever the day dished out.

Finished with his shower, Jeff came in and looked through her closet, remembering he'd left some clothes there early in the summer. He found a white button-down long-sleeved shirt and a pair of khaki pants. Lucky for him, he'd worn his black boots with his tux to the gala, so he could wear them again today.

Just as he was getting dressed, he heard Luz cry out, "Oh, no, no, no!" He hurried out to see what was going on. She was sobbing now, sitting on the sofa with the newspaper spread out in front of her on the coffee table. The front page read, "Famous winemaker Slattery dies at Charity Gala." There were two full columns of coverage, and the story continued on the back page of the front section. The society pages featured a small mention headlined, "Former debutante inherits Chateau La Mer."

Luz looked up, tears coursing down her cheeks, a tissue in her hand, "I can't believe it. I hope they called Sara last night. This is a horrible way to find out a loved one has died."

Jeff checked his phone, thinking they might have called them last night, but there were no calls or texts. Luz looked at hers too but found no messages.

"I guess we aren't meeting at the hospital after all," Luz said.

"You get dressed. I'll call Clint and Michelle and see what's going on. Probably Sara will need you to take care of some of the estate stuff, so let's be ready to go in thirty minutes. We may not be going to the hospital, but I'm sure we will be going somewhere."

BARBIE O'CONNOR

CHAPTER 4

When Luz and Jeff checked in with Michelle and Clint, the group decided that Luz would meet with the estate-planning attorney, Martin Cohen, while Michelle tended to Sara. Sacha would let Paul Angel know about their partner's death.

How the newspapers had gotten the story early enough for it to be in the morning edition was a mystery, but Michelle attributed it to a nurse or orderly at the hospital who'd probably been paid for any juicy news about noteworthy patients brought in for treatment. With all the publicity interviews that had taken place before the gala, background information about Chateau La Mer would have been easy to come by on the web.

Luz and Jeff met Mr. Cohen at his downtown office, which had a view of the Alamo. Luz had been there just a few days before to meet with him and Orval Slattery. That day they didn't discuss his funeral wishes, only how he wanted the disposition of his assets to be handled.

When he entered the conference room, Mr. Cohen was holding a FedEx envelope. He dropped it dramatically on the antique oak library table. Luz was startled by the noise, and looked up at the attorney's face.

Shaking hands with Jeff and Luz, the attorney said, "I can't believe all this happened last night at the gala. Julienne and I got home late, and since I hadn't heard anything about Orval, I went to bed assuming the old guy would be hale and hearty this morning. When I heard from Clint this morning at six, I was shocked."

Both Luz and Jeff nodded in agreement. Luz said, "When I saw it in the paper this morning, I hoped Sara knew beforehand."

"Yes, she's a little overwhelmed, after last night's announcement and then her grandfather's death. So, we have a lot to go over today. Sara called me earlier and told me I could share every detail with you. I have a faxed letter signed by her as well, so let's get started. Let's not stand on formalities."

"Shall I wait outside while you go over everything with Luz?" Jeff asked.

"No, Sara said you needed to know what was going on as well. Something about Sonoma and the race weekend. That she was going to need as many friends on her side as she could muster."

Martin's tone grew even more serious as he said, looking at each of them soberly, "Something you need to know that is not for public knowledge: Luz, Jeff, I need you to promise you will not breathe a word of this to anyone."

"I promise," Jeff said. Luz echoed his pledge.

"The police contacted me early this morning—I mean early, right after I heard from Clint—to let me know that the doctors who reviewed Orval's case after he died thought cause of death was not right for a man of his age. The lab tests they did on Orval's body indicated that there was an excessive amount of alcohol in his body. I'm not talking about wine or whiskey alcohol; I'm talking about ethanol. They think it somehow was mixed in with the wine he drank, and *only* the wine he drank. They called the hotel to see if they could pick up the bottle off the podium and the ones at the head table. They're examining them for traces of ethyl alcohol."

Luz and Jeff looked at each other.

Jeff said, "So that's why they were asking about how the wine got to the dinner and how we knew each other. Ethyl alcohol is in racing fuel. And it's a gasoline additive."

"That information isn't going to be released to the public, but the police are operating on the assumption that he was murdered, and they're looking at everyone who was at that dinner, and anyone who benefited from his death, so keep an eye on Sara and anyone else you run into."

"I'm stunned," Luz said. "Orval Slattery murdered! Who would want to do that? And why?"

"Luz, we are all suspects. We were all at that party. The only guy not at the party who might have a motive was Paul Angel, and according to the information you gave the doctors last night, he packs the wine that goes with Orval to these events," Martin said. "But let's shift gears now. We have a lot of preparations to make for the funeral."

"Let's start with the basics. Orval wanted a funeral service appropriate to him. He wanted it to take place at Mission San Jose and wanted the choir from that parish to sing at the service. He wanted a wake to be held here in San Antonio at the Argyle Club, with his closest friends in attendance, after the funeral. He wanted to be cremated and have his ashes scattered over the Chateau La Mer vineyards, but only after the harvest. And finally, he wanted to have another wake for his friends in the wine country."

Luz made notes, including the name of the funeral homes in San Antonio and Napa Valley, and the location of the cloisonné urn Orval had already purchased and selected to house his ashes until they could be scattered.

"Luz, you know we spent most of last week working on Orval's estate plan, and you were a witness to the very few minor changes he made through the codicil we added to his testamentary documents," Martin said.

Luz nodded and waited, since she heard hesitancy in his voice. Jeff sat up straight, sensing there was more to come.

Martin grabbed the FedEx envelope he had dropped on the desk and pulled the zip tab to open it. "This was sent from Napa two days ago, with Chateau La Mer and Orval Slattery listed as the sender." He slid the papers out of the envelope and laid them out in the middle of the table for Luz and Jeff to see.

"I didn't want to open this without witnesses present, since I am not sure what Orval could be sending us that I don't already have. People making estate plans are known to change their minds, but Orval always seemed so sure of his decisions once he'd wrestled with each issue."

Martin read the documents carefully while Jeff and Luz waited, watching him intently. At last Martin spoke again: "This is a codicil, naming Paul Angel as trustee over the trust Orval created to hold the remaining shares of Chateau La Mer that will ultimately go to Sara." He pushed the papers across the table to Luz.

Luz looked puzzled as she read. "Why would he do this? He just expressed his confidence in her in front of over five hundred people at the dinner last night. I don't understand."

"Nor do I," Martin agreed. "It looks more suspicious by the minute." From a separate file he pulled out the documents Orval Slattery had signed in front of Luz and compared the signature. There were similarities, but without a professional opinion he could not really say whether Orval signed them or the signature was a forgery.

"Why would he FedEx these if he was flying in so soon after executing them? Why didn't he just bring them to you? And anyway, who drafted this for him?" Luz asked.

Martin compared the new codicil with the earlier one Orval had signed, the one Luz had witnessed. The "new" one was identical in wording, with one significant difference: the new one named Paul Angel as the trustee; the old one had specified that Sara would serve as her own.

"Luz, he could have just copied it himself, or had his secretary do so, and then sent it to me. I don't know the people who witnessed it. One is Fred Bowman, and the other, looks like a Maurine Henry, maybe a secretary? But I know his secretary," said Martin, sounding puzzled. "Her name is Leticia Brown."

He picked up the phone and dialed the office in Napa. Martin recognizing Leticia's voice when she answered.

"Orval Slattery's office," she said, her voice breaking at the last syllable.

"Leticia? It's Martin Cohen, Orval's attorney in San Antonio."

"Oh, Martin! It's so terrible what happened to Mr. Slattery. I just can't believe it. It is so sad. How is his granddaughter doing?"

"Sara is with her aunt and uncle, Michelle and Clint Amberson. Right now, we are working on the funeral arrangements. Leticia, did you prepare a FedEx package for Mr. Slattery a few days ago?"

"No, I've been on vacation for the past week. When I heard the news this morning, I came in to work, since I suppose there will be a lot to do. I understand that Ms. Slattery will be taking his place. When will the funeral be? I so much want to be there," Leticia said, beginning to cry.

"I am so sorry for your loss, Leticia. You worked for him for a long time. There will be two funerals, though, one here in San Antonio, and then another after the harvest in Napa."

"That's good to hear, Mr. Cohen. I'm glad I'll be able to attend one of them." She paused. "Oh, I've been wondering, what should I do with the keys?"

"What keys?" Cohen asked.

"The ones to Mr. Slattery's house and his office."

Cohen thought about it.

"Make sure Mr. Slattery's office is locked, and his house too. Please wait until Ms. Slattery gets there, and then give her the keys. Don't give them to anyone else. If you have a safe, then I would leave them there until she arrives. I believe she'll be there in a week or so. I'll ask her to call you and let you know when to expect her. Thanks, Leticia."

After he hung up, Cohen took a closer look at the FedEx envelope. The sender's address was hand-printed, rather than machine-printed like most corporate prefilled forms would be. He said, "Something's not quite right here. I'm going to have a professional check the signature on this new codicil, and look into where the FedEx package was shipped from earlier in the week. I'll also check on Orval's schedule and find out where he was every day for the last week. His pilot may have some of the information we need."

He went on, "I'll touch base with Sara and Michelle about the funeral arrangements. We'll worry about Napa later. Isn't there a big race event sometime soon?"

Jeff answered. "Yes, Chateau La Mer puts on a very important fundraiser in Napa for their county charities. This may put a damper on those festivities. I'll be leaving early next week with our cars and team to get out there for practice and qualifying."

Luz sighed, realizing that Jeff would be gone again, but then recovered, knowing she'd be going out there with Michelle and Sara the following week.

"Luz, will you be going out there along with the team?" Martin asked. "I'd really like your help. Who is Paul Angel, anyway?"

Luz explained about the history of Chateau La Mer and the friendship of the three men who had created the illustrious

35

vineyard and winery.

"I'm sure he's a great guy. Obviously knows his winemaking," Martin said. "But I'm worried that now he controls more stock than either of the other two owners. With the takeover bids Orval made me aware of, all of which he's refused, I'm concerned that Paul Angel might accept one."

"I don't know anything about these takeover bids. Orval never mentioned them," Luz said, her voice full of concern.

"Yes, there have been several, but Orval and, I assume, all of his partners have refused them. But they aren't getting any younger. A lot of the big wineries have been taken over by conglomerates now, so they are one of the few valuable boutique wineries still in business that is privately owned," Martin said.

He leaned forward. "See if you can find out how the other partner stands on a takeover. And I guess you'd better tell him about the new codicil. Let Sara know too. Or I can if you'd rather I do it."

"No, I'll tell them. If they need more details, then I'll get them to call you. The other partner is Sacha Bernard. He owns wineries in France and a Formula International auto racing team," Luz explained.

"Yes, Chateau Bernard. One of my favorites, very delicious, but quite expensive. And a Formula International team, very interesting. Another racing connection. So now I understand where the fundraising event during the Indy car weekend comes into play. All interesting people in big-money businesses," Martin said.

At the end of his rumination he looked at her. "Before you

go, Luz, here are the keys to Orval's townhouse and the one in Napa. Like I said before, you'll find the urn at the townhouse here on the fireplace mantel. According to his will, Sara inherits both houses. Please let her know that Leticia also has a set of keys to the house in Napa and to Orval's office. I really would like you to be with her when she goes to both houses and enters his office for the first time. Can you possibly do that for me and for her?"

Luz took the keys, looking at the ornate silver fob of a dove made by a local silversmith who specialized in religious jewelry for everyday use. Then she met the lawyer's eyes again. "I'll help Sara however I can, Martin. You can count on that. You have my cell and email, so please keep me posted on what you find out about the signature and the package."

"You'll hear from me first," he said, shaking her hand and then Jeff's as they prepared to leave his office.

BARBIE O'CONNOR

CHAPTER 5

It rained the day of Orval Slattery's funeral.

"He would have appreciated the rain, thinking of how essential it was for his precious vines to grow," Sacha Bernard said in his eulogy, during which he shared the story of the three men who came together in the vineyard in the middle of the war, and explained how they grew their business as partners who were like brothers to one another. He read a short essay by Paul Angel, who sent his regrets. He was supervising the harvest that had just begun, starting with the pinot noir grapes needed for their sparkling wine cuvée known as L'Étoile du Mer.

After the service, with the ashes cradled in the cloisonné urn, now carefully wrapped in tissue in a box covered in emerald-green silk peau d'soie, Sara tearfully hugged each one of her friends and extended family. They adjourned to the private Argyle Club where stories were told and memories shared. Martin Cohen took Luz aside and guided her into a small private room where two members of the local police force, Detective Boone and his partner, waited.

"It's been confirmed. Mr. Slattery was poisoned. We are not going to make it public yet. Nor are we going to share the type of poison used with the general public. Whoever did this was able to slip the poison into the wine glass beforehand and knew how to do it.

All the bottles on the tables for the guests, normal-size bottles, 750 milliliter bottles, were fine and unaffected," said the tall, dark-haired, rail-thin detective, Travis Boone.

"That explains why Sacha didn't get poisoned," Luz said. "I handed him a glass from our table after his was broken and spilled."

"Yes, we asked Mr. Bernard for his shirt with the wine stain on it. The toxicology reports reflected a large amount of ethyl alcohol in the wine spilled on his shirt."

"We suspect someone in the winery may have doctored the wine, probably Mr. Angel, as he would have benefited most from both his partners dying. However, there is also the possibility that Ms. Slattery may have been involved. And then there is the chance that Mr. Bernard, who through both his wine connections and racing contacts could easily have added racing fuel to the wine, spilled his own glass purposely," said Detective Boone, flipping through his notebook. "The hand-blown glasses. They were given to the two men that night, right?"

"Yes, that's right. I remember handing the presentation box to Julienne Cohen about thirty minutes before we were seated for dinner," Luz said. "She opened it right in front of me to look at the design."

"And then what happened to the glasses? How did they end up on the podium?" Boone asked her.

Luz thought about it for a moment, and then Martin Cohen said, "Didn't you hand them to Sara?"

Luz nodded her head, then said hesitantly, "Yes, I handed the box to her. She knew how Orval liked everything arranged when he made toasts."

"So, it would have been easy for her or maybe for you to slip a little something into one or both of the glasses?" Boone said, "Right?"

Luz thought about the silver perfume bottle and then realized Boone was trying to railroad her into saying something she didn't know to be true, something that was pure speculation. She looked directly at him and said, "I really don't know what happened and I really can't say."

"Any one of the owners could be involved in the death of Mr. Slattery," said Boone, emphatically.

"But I can't imagine they would have wanted to do that," Luz said. "They've been partners for so many years."

"Ms. Dane, please. You are Luz Dane, the proprietor of L.M. Dane L.L.C., the investment advisory firm?" Boone asked, staring at her in a disconcerting way.

"Yes, I'm Luz Dane," she said, unnerved, as the detective took in her appearance, looking her up and down, taking note of her body language.

"You managed Mr. Slattery's money, right?"

Luz nodded and waited to hear what he had to say.

"OK, so you know that he was leaving his money to his granddaughter, and you probably also knew that if all three of the partners died, then she would end up in control of the whole shooting match, right?"

Her eyes widened, and she shook her head. "No, I didn't know she was in that position."

"Certainly, you knew that there had been several offers to buy out the winery, right? You keep on top of the stock market. Haven't you noticed how many of the big conglomerates are adding liquor and wine companies to their portfolios? Why not Chateau, Chateau, what is it called"—he flipped quickly through his notes—"ah, here it is, Chateau La Mer. Why not Chateau La Mer?"

Luz paled as she thought about the ramifications of the detective's words. Why did she feel so defensive, like he was accusing her of masterminding this whole situation? Why didn't she know any more than she did? As she thought about it, she realized that the less she said, the better. As if reading her mind, Martin Cohen stepped in.

"Detective Boone, I think you've shared a lot of important information with us all today. But all these people are grieving. His memorial service ended just an hour ago," Martin said, moving between Luz and the detective. "Let these people have some peace, please."

Realizing that the tension in the room had risen and that he needed the help of these insiders to make it easier to navigate the wine and racing arena, Detective Boone joked, "Well, I for one, am going to be careful what wine I'm drinking, and I would advise the same of everyone who has any involvement with Chateau La Mer or the racing business right now."

His attempt at levity did not bring the effect he'd hoped for: in fact, Luz shrank into herself in an attempt to get away from his physical presence. Her natural protectiveness of the people who mattered to her gave her the inner strength to say, "Detective Boone, why don't you come to the race in Sonoma? You can get the lay of the land, and hopefully find out who planned and executed this murder."

What had begun as a question had ended up sounding more like a challenge. Luz stood up a little taller and added, "The Ambersons and Sara Slattery and I will be flying out tomorrow for preparations for the charity events sponsored by Chateau La Mer, and for the race itself, which is this coming weekend. Jeff Harwood and the team are leaving in the transporter tomorrow as well. Sacha Bernard is flying out tomorrow, too. If you arrive by Friday, I'm sure you will have time to figure out who murdered Orval Slattery before the race is over on Sunday afternoon."

With that Luz reached out to shake hands with Detective Boone, nodded goodbye to Martin Cohen, and swept out of the room. When she retrieved her raincoat from the hall closet, she saw Jeff out of the corner of her eye, made the "wind it up" signal with her index finger, walked out to the porte cochere, and waited for him to join her.

When Jeff saw her, Luz had that steely, angry-like-thunder look in her eye: he knew that look meant there was no stopping her from walking out of the building. Before leaving the reception, he said goodbye to Sara, Michelle, Clint, and Sacha, saying he'd see them at the end of the week in Sonoma.

Luz was breathing deeply as she stood under the green awning smelling the welcome freshness of the rain. Her beige raincoat was open at the front, her curly black hair cascading down the back. She held her shoulders back and her chin up, waiting for the next ugly surprise she'd have to defend against.

Jeff came up behind her, said her name to let her know he was there, and put his arm around her waist, hugging her to him.

"I don't know what they said to you in there, but I'm sure none of it's true or as bad as you think it might be. Try to let it go, Luz. It has nothing to do with you," he said softly.

Luz looked at him, sadness in her eyes. "It wasn't supposed to be like this, Jeff. He was supposed to die like other old men, in his sleep, at home in bed, not this way."

"Let's go home. Take a nap. Forget about all this sadness. It's great weather to be in bed together," Jeff said, raising his eyebrow as he tried to cheer her up. "I'm leaving tomorrow and we'll be apart for a few days, which will seem like forever, so let's make the best of today now, OK?"

Luz leaned into Jeff as they walked toward the car. He was right, now was now, and later in the week she'd have time to figure out what was happening at Chateau La Mer.

CHAPTER 6

On the way to the airport, Luz thought about how different this trip was going to be than she had planned. Originally it was expected to be a lively jaunt, with Orval Slattery providing the private tours and hosting the charity events. Now there were murder suspects to eliminate, creating tension and complications. This morning Jeff had told her that she'd cried out in her sleep again and that he was worried about the time they would be apart.

When dawn slipped into the bedroom the two of them were spooned together, his hands on her breasts, his hardness between her buttocks. Their desire led them on an intense session of lovemaking that left both of them breathless, glowing with sweat, and late to shower, change, and get to the plane.

It was a short drive Jeff had made many times before, and fortunately Luz had packed her clothes, laptop, client list, and purse the night before. With her wet hair in a French braid, dressed in jeans and a long-tailed white shirt, Luz was think-ing about the few days they would be separated. Jeff would be in the team bus, taking care of his business over the three days it took to get to Sonoma.

Why she wasn't riding with him, she didn't know, except that now she was going to help Sara, one of her best clients, with what was now one of her largest investments. Luz prac-ticed a concierge style of money management that required her to be there for her clients not only as a consultant for their traditional investments, like stocks and bonds, but for their overall financial planning and whatever else that entailed. Her network of attorneys, accountants, and trust officers en-abled her to employ a broad vision for her clients, making it very interesting and exciting for her. Each day was different from any other.

At the airport, Jeff helped Luz with her bags, making sure that she had her laptop and purse in the cabin and that her clothes made it into the cargo hold. Then he gave her a long embrace on the tarmac, with a lingering kiss. Finally he let her go, "Goodbye."

"I'll see you in a few days," Luz said. "Text me and let me know where you are on the highway, please." Memories of her parents' death in a car crash haunted her whenever she knew he was going to be on a long road trip.

"Of course. And I plan on calling you too, so remember to answer the phone!"

Luz frequently turned her phone off or silenced the ring-tone when she was in a meeting or working on a project. Often she would forget to turn it back on for an hour or two afterward, so she often missed calls from Jeff.

"Yes!" she answered, pulling out her phone out to show him that the ringer was on.

"You'll be turning that off in just a minute, before you take off, so when you get to Sonoma, please check it!" Jeff laughed at her, gave her one more hug, and gently pushed her toward the plane stair.

Michelle and Sara were already ensconced in their seats, leaving Luz to ride facing backward, beside Clint. Fortunately, as a child she had loved being in the very back seat of her grandmother's old station wagon, seeing the road fall away from her as the trusty car barreled down the highway. Seeing where she'd been helped her reflect on where she was going.

As the plane taxied to the end of the runway to turn around for takeoff, Luz watched Jeff return to his SUV and leave the private plane area of the airport. Her heart hurt watching him go alone out the chain-link gate and take the access road to the freeway, where he joined the other cars going north toward Boerne, heading to the shop that housed the team headquarters. She watched his SUV blend into traffic, and kept watching until she lost sight of him.

"You love that boy, don't you?" Clint asked her softly.

Luz turned to him, her eyes moist, and nodded. "Yes. Yes, I do, probably more than I should. If it weren't for all this estate stuff for Sara, I would have gone with him in the team RV, but here I am."

"Luz, this was the choice you made when you decided it was time to leave Emerson York. I will never forget that day," Clint said.

Michelle, listening in, laughed. "Oh, yes, that was some day. When your boss criticized you for getting all that publicity for the team while you were working at Indy. And then when he said it was the last time he wanted to hear your name, our name and that of Emerson York, used in the same sentence."

Sara put down the magazine she'd been reading and listened, intrigued by this story she had never heard before.

"You left the office in the middle of the morning, cancelled all your appointments, and drove straight out to our place in Boerne in record time, as far as I could tell," Clint said. "You were spitting mad when you walked in the door."

"Yes, I was," Luz said. "I had opened new accounts, increased commissions, trained the administrative assistants, helped the new hires pass their securities exams, and been a great team player, and no one in management gave me any credit for my work."

"Yes, and you know what happened?" Clint said, "Emerson York went into bankruptcy because of that mortgage bond business. And weeks before the news broke and their stock tanked, you got rid of all those shares you'd bought through the stock purchase plan—gave them to charity. You are much smarter than that hypocritical manager you had. He was always sucking up to us while treating you like dirt."

"Now you've got your own firm. Your very best clients, like Sara, are still working with you, and lots of new folks were referred to you during the financial crisis. And you get to work for us on race weekends!" Michelle said, patting Luz on the arm.

"Your mom and dad would be proud of you, Luz. You've

done a lot of good for a lot of people, and now it's time for you to live your life like you want it to be," Clint said. "Life is not a dress rehearsal, after all."

Luz smiled. "Yes, Mom always said, 'Live each day like it is your last' and 'Regrets are what make old age a sad place to be.' I am glad to be here right now with all of you. Thank you for believing in me. It gave me the confidence to start something for myself."

"We knew it might be hard for you leaving the place where you basically grew up from a young lady to a grown adult woman," Clint said.

"Yes," Michelle said, "but we also knew that you'd have your pick of the best clientele even if you work out of a pickup truck. You're that good and that dedicated to your clients."

Sara joined in. "This is such an interesting story. My grandfather told me Luz would be a good woman to network with, since she knew what it was like to be in a man's world. At that point I didn't quite understand what he meant, but now I do."

"Sara, I've learned a lot from Michelle, too," Luz said. "It's almost like you have to have a mask or an alter ego when you are in the business world. Some men, present company excluded, take women at face value. They just objectify or belittle us. You have to be strong and confident when you go into any business meeting where women will be in the minority. And, of course, you have to do your homework.".

"And speaking of homework," she continued, "that overbearing Detective Boone wants me to come up with all kinds of information so he can solve your grandfather's murder. Sara, you and I are going to be spending a lot of time together, and I am going to be asking questions like crazy. Please don't take anything personally. If I can get this figured out before he gets here Friday, then it will be a lot better for you." Luz looked directly at Sara, then opened her laptop and found the new spreadsheet she'd made—the one with her list of things to learn.

"Sure, like what? Ask away," Sara said, putting down her magazine.

"OK. Well, first, tell me what you knew about your grandfather's will before he died."

"Over the last ten years he gave me shares in the company that owned Chateau La Mer, some estate planning gimmick Martin Cohen recommended. He said he was also creating a trust that would contain all his remaining shares of the company. I would be named the trustee, so I would control all his shares after he was gone. He said it was what Martin Cohen recommended to save on estate tax. He never said anything about anyone else serving as trustee," Sara stated matter-of-factly.

"Do you know what Sacha Bernard and Paul Angel planned to do with their shares on their death?" Luz asked. Though looking distractedly at her computer, she was taking careful note of Sara's tone of voice and body language.

"I have no clue. Why would I know anything about that?" Sara asked, clearly mystified by the question.

"Just wondered if Orval had shared anything with you, since they'll be your new partners." Luz answered. "How about anything about anyone trying to buy out the winery, like a big corporation or anything like that?"

"No, he never said anything about anyone trying to buy the winery. I can't imagine he would have sold his shares anyway," Sara said defensively. "He loved Chateau La Mer.".

"Wait a minute, Luz," Michelle interrupted. "These are really serious questions, and I don't like what you are insinuating."

"I don't like it either, but I have to know. It's a lot better for me to ask her than Detective Boone. He was ready to arrest all of us at the reception yesterday. That was why I left without saying goodbye—I was just spitting mad."

"Then you can imagine how I felt when I got this in the mail," Sara said. She tried to hand Luz an envelope, but Michelle quickly grabbed it and opened it.

Michelle frowned. "This is a letter from Paul Angel. He expresses his condolences, and then he says that Orval selected him as her trustee to manage the winery until she turned thirty years of age and that he looks forward to seeing her soon in Sonoma. He signed it himself," Michelle said.

She continued, "I just don't understand this document. Orval said Sara would be stepping into his shoes at the winery. All five hundred guests at the gala heard him—he said it that night, right before he died. I can't imagine what made him change his mind."

"It is hard to understand," Luz said. "And there is one more thing. This is hard for me to ask you, Sara, but tell me about the silver perfume cylinder."

Sara looked down at her purse and started digging through it, then looked accusingly at Luz. "Where is it? It's not here. Did you take it?"

"I found it at the hospital. Under a table. After everything fell out of your purse the other night."

"What did you do with it?"

"It smelled like almonds and alcohol."

Michelle watched the interchange between the two young women, and as it escalated, she thought about the information shared.

"Almonds...arsenic. Alcohol...in the wine," she said, worriedly, "you can't seriously think Sara..."

"That night I didn't know what to think. I gave it to the detective. I hope there is nothing to it," Luz responded.

Sara was furious. "How dare you? Why didn't you give it back to me?"

Luz watched Sara, wondering what she was so upset about if she was innocent. Michelle was lost in thought.

"Tell me, Sara," Luz said. "If you need legal representation, now is the time to do something about it."

Tears rolled down her face. Sara looked from Michelle to Luz and then back again to Michelle. "It was after his last stroke. When he was recuperating. He said, he said, he never wanted to be kept alive if he was brain dead."

Sara wept, blowing her nose, as she thought about her vibrant grandfather and how weak and frail he was after the first stroke. Michelle teared up too, looking across at Clint.

"So he mixed up this concoction and put it in the atomizer and told me to have it with me whenever we were together, so if he needed it, he could use it. He said he'd know. He'd know when the time was right."

Clint nodded in agreement, patted Sara's hand, and said,

"Honey, I understand exactly what he wanted and why. Growing old is not easy."

Luz felt like she'd been beating a puppy as she watched Sara keening with the pain of losing her grandfather.

Luz sat up straight, stretched her neck from side to side, and considered this new information from Sara. If she was telling the truth, then only Orval's prints would be on the glass vial inside the atomizer. Hopefully that was the case.

After thinking about how the detectives might twist that information, Luz said, "I have my work cut out for me. Sara, I will find out who murdered your grandfather before any damage is done to your reputation, or Chateau La Mer's."

BARBIE O'CONNOR

CHAPTER 7

In the small booth at the back of the truck stop diner just a few miles outside Napa, Roger Schneider read the current issue of *Speed News*. A yellow gimme-cap embroidered with a black bird was pulled down low over his eyes, concealing his face. He read a feature about the Amberson-Harwood team being the favorite to win the Indy series championship. Farther down the page was an article about Sacha Bernard, his Formula International team, and his business interest in Chateau La Mer. The article speculated that Bernard would come to the Sonoma track looking for new American talent to take to Europe for testing and possible sponsorship for another team in the Formula International auto racing series. Just as he finished the article, a man slid into the seat opposite him and asked the waitress for a cup of coffee.

"Hey, Schneider. Remember me, your favorite West Coast playmate?" said the balding man with a slick salesman's demeanor.

"It's about time. You're over thirty minutes late. I don't have all day. I've got to get back to the track for practice. It looks like my old team is going to sew up the championship and I'm going to be out of business unless this scheme of yours works," Schneider said harshly, his face set in an ugly scowl.

"It took a little longer to make the switch. I had to stall the granddaughter, and now this other guy, some Frenchman, wants to come see things, and putting them off until everything is set up has been a trial. But I'm ready for them now, so don't worry about a thing," he said as he perused the menu. "Do you know if the pie here is any good?"

"I don't have time for you to have pie. I've got to get back. You know what to do, right?"

"Yes, we've gone over it a hundred times. I'll take care of everything. Now go to the track. Practice, qualify, and win. I've got everything taken care of at Chateau La Mer."

"By the way, have you heard from Girard Morel lately?" Schneider asked. "I need another hot tip from him. Running a race team is not cheap."

"Hey, he made you a millionaire once or twice over. What are you complaining about?" the bald man responded.

"I'm hemorrhaging money. I've got to win this race—my future depends on it," Schneider said, as he exited the booth, laying money on the table for his meal.

"I told you. I've got it all under control. Don't worry about a thing." The bald man took a gulp of coffee.

"I sure hope so," Roger said. "See ya around. Good luck with the CLM deal."

Schneider got in his truck and drove the winding road through the mountains between Napa and Sonoma, thinking the whole way about how he was going to get from Indy racing to Formula International racing.

After the fiasco at Indy, when that busybody Luz Dane forced him out of the Amberson team over a little thing like using the Amberson funds to outfit his team, Blackbird Racing, Roger Schneider was looking for any way to get ahead. Already he was thinking about the carousel of turns on the Sonoma track, far from the pit road, where it would be easy to hide a tire failure that would spin an open-wheel car off the track and down a treacherous hillside, leading to a "Did Not Finish," or DNF, for that driver and team.

He'd heard rumors about Christi Cole considering a leap to Formula International, with Jeff Harwood looking to make that transition with her. Schneider wondered how it was that only last April Christi had been a rookie, and Jeff's own open-wheel car had been destroyed, and now the two were the darlings of the Indy circuit. Meanwhile, Schneider's team and drivers plodded along, finishing in the middle to the end of the pack at each track no matter how hard he tried to ace out the competition. He was the one with the family pedigree in auto racing. Growing up with a father who built chassis for stock car racers, Roger had lived in garages his entire life. He knew all of the mechanics worth knowing, famous drivers saw him grow up working on their cars, and almost all the team owners had hired him and fired him over the years.

This was his last chance before he faded into the background of this sport. Once he got a reputation as a mediocre player in auto racing, it would diminish the amount of sponsorship money he'd earn, further limiting the quality of the equipment and the competence of the team members he could recruit.

Blackbird Racing had to win this race, to show that he, Roger Schneider, had the wherewithal to put together a team that could triumph on a road-course, which was the predominant racing circuit for Formula International. The man who was bringing the money to the table for everything Schneider needed for this one big weekend had assured him that everything was going to go as planned.

As he rounded the last S-turn on the mountain, Schneider encountered another truck coming toward him, driving in the wrong lane. He yelled, "Hey, watch where you're going!" and leaned on the horn of his truck.

Pulling close to the edge of the road to avoid a collision, Schneider looked over to see a deep chasm below him, his tires slipping on the slick marbled edge of the hillside. Feeling fear deep in the pit of his stomach, he let out a deep breath as he corrected. He missed the oncoming truck by inches.

The hairs on his arm stood straight up and his heart beat faster as he drove down the gentle slope that led into Sonoma. At the nearest opportunity he pulled over, wiped the damp flop sweat off his brow, and caught his breath. He'd never been so close to going over the edge before, and the thought of what would have happened if he'd gone over the side of the cliff nauseated him. Looking around at the calm serenity around him as autumn and the harvest settled in, Roger Schneider started his truck and drove on toward the raceway, hoping his plans would bring him the outcome he wanted, a future in racing at the highest levels in Formula International.

CHAPTER 8

Shortly after their plane touched down, while they were gathering their belongings and sorting out what went into which car, another jet taxied down the runway, heading for the same fixed base operator, or FBO, where the Amberson jet parked. As it got closer, Luz and her friends could see on its fuselage the livery design that included a fleur-de-lys, the logo for the Chateau Bernard winery, and that of the Formula International Racing team. It was not surprising that they would be using the same FBO to supply their planes with fuel, hangar space, and maintenance: this operator was known for its efficiency, its quality service, and the luxury amenities they offered their clientele.

"It's Sacha!" Michelle exclaimed.

Clint scowled. "You just saw him at Orval's funeral, Michelle. You act like you haven't seen him in years. All along he planned to join us in Sonoma. He and Sara have business to take care of, and they are hosting that fussy dinner party you are so excited about" he said crankily.

Luz watched the exchange for a moment and realized she had never seen this couple, one she thought of as a pair of lovebirds, bicker in private, much less in public. What was going on?

Sara glanced at Luz, put a finger to her lips to advise silence, and raised her eyebrow in the direction of Sacha Bernard as he debarked from his plane.

"Michelle, Clint, we are together again!" Sacha said, putting his arm around Michelle and hugging her to him. At the same time, he shook hands with Clint.

"Luz, so good to see you. Sara and I are counting on you to solve the mystery of Orval's death," Sacha said as he patted Sara on the shoulder. "Certainly that policeman has no clue to what is going on."

Luz was startled by the cockiness exuding from Sacha Bernard, but she attributed it to his reputation and accomplishments. He was used to things being taken care of for him and being handled with discretion and good taste.

Three cars appeared by the planes: a classic Mustang convertible for Clint and Michelle, a Bentley convertible for Sacha Bernard, and a little red BMW convertible for Luz and Sara. Since Sara was inheriting her grandfather's home and all it contained, she just needed a ride there and the opportunity to get settled.

With a few days to go before practice and qualifying at the track, Luz had time to learn more about the Chateau La Mer partners, and especially Paul Angel. After she took Sara to

Orval's house, Luz would check into the same small hotel in Sonoma where Clint and Michelle were staying, located fairly close to the track.

On the drive to her grandfather's house, Sara gave Luz directions, but did not say anything else about Orval or the winery. Luz concentrated on her driving, all the while thinking about the three partners of one of the most famous wineries in the world.

Before leaving for the wine country, Luz had researched Paul Angel, downloading what few pictures and files she could find that said anything about his background. It was odd that with the social media presence most businesses required to be successful, she found only old publicity photos from when the winery first broke ground, and none of them featured Paul Angel.

Luz researched Orval Slattery as well, thinking she might find some unexpected detail that would explain the confusion regarding the trust and Sara's inheritance. On reading about the founding of Chateau La Mer, Luz was surprised that Orval's partner, Sacha Bernard, was not named the trustee. Bernard was the Frenchman who owned one of the stellar houses in Bordeaux, Chateau Bernard, and it was Bernard who had originally proposed that the three men merge their knowledge to create an American wine with a French pedigree.

Sacha Bernard was well known in both racing and wine circles: he owned several other famous French vineyards in addition to Chateau Bernard, along with a champagne house that regularly sponsored a Formula International team. His presence in Sonoma would also garner notice from the business media and social circles. The publicity photos for the race team only hinted at how handsome he was in person. His carefully trimmed mustache set off his chiseled features, giving him a cultured, metropolitan look. Now that Luz had met him, she understood why, in every photo, Sacha Bernard was surrounded by beautiful women.

When she last met with Martin Cohen, Luz had created a list of the items to be discussed with the two remaining partners, Sacha Bernard and Paul Angel, including the future plans for the winery, the role Sara would play in its management and how Sara would eventually assume control of the inheritance left to her by her grandfather, Orval.

Sara, in her own right, had a one-sixth interest in the winery; the trust in question also had a one-sixth interest; and Sacha Bernard and Paul Angel each had a one-third interest. Now, as both trustee and part owner, Paul Angel controlled half of the shares in Chateau La Mer.

Luz asked to be included in that meeting, leaving Sara to ask whatever questions she wanted, knowing that Luz would get the answers that Martin insisted he needed to complete his work on behalf of the Slattery estate. While Sara and Luz were meeting with the other two partners, Martin Cohen planned to file the Texas will for probate, allowing Sara access to Orval Slattery's personal assets managed by L. M. Dane LLC, along with any other property not included in the trust. Simultaneously, he would research the trust utilizing his contacts in California to clarify Sara's position as the ultimate heir of Orval Slattery's portion of the famous Chateau La Mer winery.

"Turn right here," Luz heard Sara say, right before she

needed to take the tight turn into a driveway that started up-hill and then transitioned into a descending, winding road for about one hundred yards, where it stopped at a home situated on a rocky plateau-like outcropping.

When they arrived at Orval Slattery's home, Sara started to open the car door, then stopped, sat back, and turned to Luz with tears in her eyes. "I can't believe he won't be here when I walk in. He was always here to greet me when I came out here in the summer to work at the winery."

"It is really hard to lose someone you love, someone who has been like another father to you. I know what you are going through, Sara," Luz said, squeezing the younger woman's hand. "At least I'm here, and your Aunt Michelle is here. You aren't alone. You'll get through it. I've found it helps to cry a lot of tears, drink a lot of cold water and a moderate amount of wine, and eat a lot of chocolate."

Sara slipped out of the car, took a look at the house and garden, and saw that pretty much everything was the same as it had been the last time she visited her grandfather. Walking toward the wrought iron gate that led to a xeriscaped patio, Sara turned to Luz and said, "Thank you for being here for me."

As they walked into the garden, Luz saw the pink and purple lantana, the lemon-yellow blooms of an esperanza bush, and a Mexican Olive tree with its white blossoms shading the patio. Sara hesitated at the door, fumbling with the key, then turned to Luz. "Would you open it? I just can't. There was always someone here to greet me. Walking into an empty house..."

Luz took the keys with the silver dove fob and, as she unlocked the door, asked, "Before I open this, do you know if there is an alarm? And, if there is, what's the code? I'd hate to set it off and have another set of policemen to deal with here."

"Oh, yeah, right," Sara said, as she thought for a moment. "Yes, I remember it. You can go ahead now."

Entering the cool, tiled entryway, Sara turned to the wall on the right and found the alarm keypad. She entered the code she'd memorized years before, and happily the security system accepted it and welcomed them with a "system disarmed" chirp.

Walking through the house, turning on the lights, Sara glanced around as if she expected to find some secret message left to her by her grandfather. Luz, who had never before visited Orval's Napa house, took in the museum-quality art, along with the many photos sitting on bookshelves, tables, and a grand piano: both family photographs and others of Orval with people of note.

On the piano was a photo of three men: what looked like a younger version of Orval Slattery in his World War II army uniform, Sacha Bernard in work pants and a cotton shirt, and a third man, this one wearing a kerchief around his neck and a chambray work shirt. Luz studied the photo carefully and was startled when Sara came up behind her and tapped her on the shoulder.

"I'm really feeling tired. I think I'll just take a nap now and then drop in at the winery before I meet you all later."

"Sure, I can imagine you are tired from the trip and emotionally tired, too." Luz said. "Martin wanted me to be there when you first visited your grandfather's office. Are you good with handling it on your own?"

"I'm going to have to be there on my own sometime, so it might as well be today. But Luz, is it OK if I stay with you at the hotel in Sonoma tonight? I'm not ready to spend the night here alone. Maybe in a couple of days I'll be fine with it."

Luz turned around to look at her. Sara's eyes were puffy, red, and still moist with tears.

"Of course. Whatever will make you feel more comfortable. You've been through a lot of changes in just one week. I'll let the hotel desk know to give you a key, in case I'm not there when you arrive. By the way, I don't know how to get to Sonoma, so can you get me started? Once I'm in town, I think I can find the hotel."

Sara gave her directions from the house out of Napa to Sonoma, and Luz hopped into her little rental and drove through the valley.

CHAPTER 9

On her way to Sonoma, about twenty minutes from the Slattery house on Highway 12, Luz thought about the circumstances of Orval's death, the revelation of a new trust previously unknown to his estate planning attorney, and the presence of Sacha Bernard, one of the partners in the winery.

According to Sara, Paul Angel always hand-selected the wines for any tasting or special event where Orval Slattery was the guest presenter. There had been hundreds of such events all over the country—Orval was in great demand as a speaker, and of course to have a donation of Chateau La Mer for your charity event, either to auction or to be featured in a charity tasting, was quite an accomplishment. Although he was generous, there were only so many bottles produced each year, and only so many days open on his calendar. But to have Sacha Bernard at the event for the Children's Home also was amazing, since he was equally busy and had business interests all over the world. They must have wanted the announcement about Sara joining the winery to be international news.

Then there was the question of reputation. No self-respecting winemaker, especially one with Paul Angel's reputation, would want to have the words "death" and "Chateau La Mer wine" in the same sentence. Unless of course, he wanted the winery's reputation and its value to be diminished. That only made sense if he planned to buy his partner's shares at less than market price. "Buy on bad news, sell on good" was a saying on Wall Street that might apply in this situation. Luz wondered if there was another person who might be behind this entire debacle, maybe someone unknown or even invisible to the wine-drinking community.

When she arrived in Sonoma, she suddenly felt hungry, and realized she had not eaten since she got on the plane to come to California. She decided to stop for a bite to eat before checking into the hotel.

Walking around the little square, Luz took her time, stopping to read the menus posted outside the small bistros offering everything from California cuisine to authentic Italian fare. While she was reading one menu, she heard a deep voice ask, "*Voulez vous mangé avec moi?*"

Turning toward the voice, Luz stared straight into the eyes of Sacha Bernard. He looked like he was holding his breath.

"Will you? Eat with me?" he repeated in English, smiling as he did so.

It was around two o'clock—late for an American to eat, but perfect for a Frenchman. Luz was hungry, and maybe this was her chance to learn more about the genesis of Chateau La

Mer. She knew lunch with Sacha Bernard came with its own risks, like taking up the rest of her day, since it would involve several glasses of wine, eating slowly, and lots of conversation. She would have to have a nap afterward if she was going to make it to dinner that night, much less be able to enjoy it.

"I would love to," she said brightly. She took his arm and they walked into the cozy bistro together. Sacha burst into a torrent of French, making lively conversation with the owner and securing them the best table, on a private balcony off of the wine room in the back of the restaurant. As soon as they were seated, napkins, cutlery, and glasses of champagne were placed before them, along with a charcuterie plate with paté, olives, and a few gherkins, and crusty sourdough bread with a side of softened butter.

Luz had a view of the valley and the mountains beyond from her side of the table, while Sacha Bernard looked over a vista of grapevines climbing up the adjacent hillside, laden with fruit awaiting the harvest. Luz absorbed the atmosphere and carefully scrutinized her dining companion.

First Luz glanced at his carefully manicured hands lying on the tabletop, the right one embellished with a signet ring, most likely adorned with the family crest. Then she looked up at his face, noticing the tiny crinkles at the edges of his hazel-gold eyes. A few stray gray hairs sprinkled his moustache and speckled his temples, complementing his full head of dark, wavy brown hair. He looked like a cat watching a mouse he hoped to devour. With a darting motion, Sacha reached for his glass of champagne and said, "*A votre santé!*"

Luz gave him a half-smile, looked him in the eyes, raised

her glass, and repeated the toast. Taking a small sip, she considered the wine: yeasty, buttery, with a delicate finish. Slowly she put her glass back on the table.

"You are not afraid of me?" Sacha asked, "not even a little bit?"

"What is there to be afraid of? That you will hurt me? Abuse me? Ruin my life? I don't think so, Sacha," Luz chuckled. "You are a very charming man, but you obviously want something from me, and I think we will talk about it over lunch in a very short while."

His eyebrows went up in surprise as he listened to her, then he broke the bread into pieces, spread a bit of pâté on one, and offered it to her.

"I must be losing my touch. Or you are a very smart woman," he said, looking at her confusedly as she took the bread from him and placed it on her butter plate.

"I'll let you be the judge of that as we get to know one another," Luz said, taking another sip of the delicious wine. "I assume you already ordered our lunch? I hope we are having sole, with lemon, butter, and capers."

Just as she finished speaking, two plates appeared before them, and on them were fillets of Dover sole, beautifully prepared in a lemon beurre blanc sauce accompanied by steamed asparagus and tiny new potatoes.

"Just what I wanted," Luz laughed, picking up her fork.

Sacha looked at her suspiciously, as if she were reading his mind. Then he too chuckled, and the two of them laughed out loud, sharing the joke and toasting each other again.

"Yes, you are correct. I do want something from you. So

many things happening at once, and I find myself in the middle of them, and it disturbs me."

"Such as?" Luz asked, as she put another bite of the buttery fish in her mouth.

"Orval Slattery's death. This new trust he made. Changes at the winery I know nothing about. Your little driver, Christi, who should be in Formula International Racing, but whom I never heard about before May. It is like the world turned upside down."

"Christi will prove her value at this race, and it will be up to her whether she moves on to another race series, maybe the FIR. I have no influence there," Luz stated matter-of-factly.

"But you discovered her and gave her the chance to drive. That is the story everyone tells," Sacha said emphatically, tearing off a large piece of bread and aggressively mopping up the sauce with it.

Luz went on to explain that Christi had tested with Jeff at Indy, but lost her ride with him because there was only one car to drive. After his car was destroyed and the Amberson team members jumped ship to join Roger Schneider, Luz admitted, she did convince Christi to drive for Amberson, along with Jeff's other driver, Mark Miller.

Sacha hung on her every word as she told the story of that fateful day at Indy when all she wanted to do was save the Amberson team and make it into the 500, in whatever way possible.

"*Sacrebleu*! You think fast on your feet. Maybe you want to come to Formula International and run my team?"

Luz laughed at the suggestion and, putting her hand over

his, said, "Sacha, what an invitation! Especially coming from you. You know how very prestigious it is to work with those elite FIR competitors. To reach that level would be the pinnacle of success in racing—traveling all over the world, meeting interesting people like you."

Sacha beamed at her, thinking he had won her over, only to have her add, "However, my focus right now is getting the Amberson-Harwood team through this weekend, and getting my new business successfully off the ground. Maybe later we can talk about Formula International."

When the salad plates were placed on the table, Luz asked Sacha about the comment he made about changes in the winery and the trust and Orval Slattery's death.

"Usually when I come to the wine country, I meet with the staff, review the tasting notes, walk through the fields, look at the fruit, and consult with the Chateau La Mer winemaker, Paul Angel, my longtime friend and partner. I know I have been here just a few hours, but I have not been able to reach him which is very unsatisfactory for me," Sacha said, distress filling his voice. "This winery is very important to our worldwide sales. The wine must be made precisely to complement our French wines. Our reputation is on the line. If Paul and I cannot talk face to face, it will not do, it will not work."

The wine now loosening his tongue, Sacha continued, "And then there is this other fellow…"

Luz leaned forward, curious. "What other fellow?"

"He asks me about Formula International, and whether Chateau La Mer will want to fund other race teams, like one this weekend, called, hmm, Black Crow, or Blackbird, and who else I know in France in the wine industry that wants to be involved with racing."

When she heard the name Blackbird, Luz felt a shiver crawl up her spine. It could only mean that Roger Schneider was once again on the Indy car circuit, looking for funding for his team. She hadn't yet looked at the entrant list—she hadn't had time—but she had no doubt it was Schneider. With hundreds of wineries in the Napa and Sonoma Valleys, why was he once again sniffing around a longtime Amberson sponsor?

"Luz, are you well?" Sacha asked her, putting his hand over hers.

She started when she felt the warmth of his hand and heard his concerned voice. While thinking about Schneider and his nefarious plans, Luz gazed over the calm green valley, just beginning to show the change to fall colors. She abruptly turned to look at Sacha, her face filled with pain and fear.

Quickly she shared with him all that transpired at Indy in May of that year, some of which he knew, but not all. She went on, "I researched Paul Angel on the internet, but there were no pictures anywhere of him. Nothing on the winery website or on the social media pages, not even from the Confrérie des Chevaliers du Tastevin. Nothing."

Sacha took another sip of wine and paused to choose his words. "There is something you must know about Paul. He was part of the resistance in France when he was a little boy. It is said that he killed many men, and that he believes he has enemies and families of those enemies who wish to avenge those deaths. His real name is not Paul Angel; that is the name he claimed when he came to America. My father knew him

from the war, and afterward. Paul helped resurrect our vineyards and wineries in France, and when he wanted to come to
America, we helped him do so."

"How did he kill the men during the war?" Luz asked,
holding her breath.

"He poisoned them," Sacha said softly. "He put poison in
the wine they drank."

Luz gasped; her eyes wide.

"Do not jump to conclusions, mademoiselle! When Orval
died, I saw I had work to do at Chateau La Mer. To find out the
truth."

"We are both here to discover the truth," Luz said.

Sacha nodded and looked out over the valley. Luz took a
sip of her wine. Neither spoke for quite a while. Their waiter
took away the salad plates and brought two demitasse cups of
espresso along with two small ramekins filled with chocolate
pot de crème. Sacha nodded at him as he brought cream and
sugar for their coffee.

"What if something happened to Paul? If he is dead? Or
been kidnapped? Or being blackmailed? What if he really
wanted the winery for himself, and really did poison Orval?
How would you know?" Luz asked.

"What an imagination you have! I know Paul. He would
never betray our friendship. He would never leave without
telling me. I would recognize him. I could identify him."

"But only if you could actually see him, right?" Luz posed
the question as a supposition.

"I know his voice."

"Yes, but earlier you told me you could not reach him." She

wondered whether Sacha was lying to her and had forgotten his lie.

"Yes. And I've made two meetings with him, but he has already cancelled one today, and I was told by Maurine Henry, that we would have plenty of time tomorrow to cover everything that interests me."

"So you have not been able to talk to him over the phone or in person. You have not been able to see him. And someone else whose name you do not know is asking you about sponsoring a race team," Luz summarized.

"Yes, and also when I asked Madame Henry to send me the details of the winemaking that are essential for me to know, she said Paul did not have those ready for me, yet."

"Sara said the same thing to me."

"And there is something else. See this scar, this wavy line here on my left hand." Sacha pulled back the cuff of his shirt and showed her what looked like a profile of a duck crudely inked where his thumb joined the back of his hand.

"Yes, what about it? Looks like it was drawn by a child."

"We were very young. Paul had lost his family and did not want to lose me. So we made our own tattoo. He has a matching one. When you put our fists together, it is an angel," Sacha explained to Luz.

"Oh, so there is another way to identify him once we find him."

"Yes, exactly. What did Sara tell you about Paul?"

"She said that when she asked for the answers to specific questions, he sent her information on another subject or a different topic. Most of the information coming from him is generic information that could apply to any wine. Nothing specific. She too has not been able to talk with him. Only his secretary and that manager, Fred Bowman."

"*Quel désastre*! It cannot be that Paul is dead or has left without telling me. He is not a coward. What can have happened?" Sacha fiddled with his package of Gitanes and lighted one nervously. Realizing he had forgotten his manners, he offered one to Luz, who laughed.

"Thank you, Sacha, but I don't smoke," Luz said. "So: it seems likely that Paul either is dead, has left, or has been kidnapped. We make a plan. We need to check the bank accounts to see if large sums of money have been withdrawn, and we need you to describe Paul to a sketch artist so we have an image to show others. The police need to help us."

"Not the police," Sacha said firmly. "The publicity will kill the winery."

"The news that your famous winemaker is no longer making your Chateau La Mer cabernet sauvignon may kill the winery, too!" Luz countered. "Remember, that detective from Texas is arriving in Sonoma in two days. So we have a lot to learn, and very little time."

"Yes, but the next few days... It is so important that I be here at the dinners, the winery, the events, the races. I should not be spending my time with the police, who will suspect me first of all." Sacha stubbed out his cigarette in the crystal ashtray the proprietor had brought to him the minute he lit up.

"Sacha, has it occurred to you that your life might be in danger? First Orval, now maybe Paul—who's left? You? Sara? What happens if you all die?" Luz asked softly.

"Luz, you have a very suspicious mind. My shares go to Sara, in trust also. And Paul has no children either, so I believe he is leaving them to her as well."

"So Sara is the ultimate beneficiary. And what if she dies after inheriting the shares from the three of you? What then?"

"The shares in the trusts we created will go to the employees if Sara dies before her twenty-fifth birthday," Sacha said.

"Oh, good. So all of you are in danger until we can find the killer," Luz said sarcastically. "And I left Sara alone in her grandfather's house."

"I do not think whoever it is will kill us all at once, Luz. But you must warn Sara, and I will be careful. We can do this. We will work on this together. We will go to the bank together. When I go to the winery, I will get you in places where you can find out what has happened to Paul. Michelle tells me that you are a very smart lady and that you helped them find their money and who took it."

"Hmmm... For this to work, no one at the winery can know that I am working with you, Sacha. See if you can access the financial accounts online, and then we can look at them together off-site. I will go over to tour the winery and look around, get a feel for what is going on. You and Sara stick to your schedule for this week." She paused, then asked, "By the way, why are you not at the winery now?"

"I was on my way there, but I wanted to have lunch with you. To ask you to help me. I saw your little car on the road, taking the turnoff to Sonoma. I thought I would follow. With the Bentley I had to drive much slower so you would not see me."

"And you noticed I was looking for a place to eat, since I was strolling through the town, reading all the menus. When I came to this restaurant, where you knew the owner, you approached me very elegantly," Luz said. "I'm flattered you think so highly of me. I hope I can help both you and Sara."

She folded her napkin, placed it on the table, and looked at her watch. "It has been a very interesting lunch, Sacha. But if we don't find out anything about Paul by Thursday, then the police will certainly get involved. You can be sure of that."

He nodded somberly. "I understand and I agree. Hopefully we can find Paul and figure out what is happening at Chateau La Mer."

CHAPTER 10

Luz parted ways with Sacha Bernard, giving him a hug and kissing him on both cheeks, then slowly drove through Sonoma to the hotel. Luz had agreed to a casual dinner with Clint, Michelle, and Sara that night, meeting at seven o'clock, so it was time to check in and take a short nap.

Pulling into the valet parking line at the lovely Inn on the Square, Luz noticed the black Mercedes AMG SLC roadster in front of her had a Chateau La Mer parking sticker on the back rear window. She gathered her portfolio and tote bag to get out of the car and watched it slip away.

Luz quickly brightened up her smile and stepped out of the car, handing her keys to the same young valet.

"Does that man work at that famous winery?" Luz asked in star struck wonder," Chateau what's-its-name?"

"Chateau La Mer. Yes, I think he's their winemaker. He tips well, but he can be a little difficult."

"Really?" Luz said. "How do you mean?"

"He's been at the winery for years, and now he does all the big money deals. Not sure what his name is, but his key chain has the initials PA. Hey, I'm Robbie, by the way. Are you checking in here? Cars are stacking up, so I need to get moving."

"Yes, I'll be around. Enjoyed the visit, Robbie. My name is Luz. See you again soon," she said, slipping him a nice tip.

Once she had settled in the room she would share that night with Sara, Luz texted her friend to give her the room number and let her know that she had already checked in. The time change and the wine from lunch had made her sleepy, so she settled in for a short nap.

As she drifted off to sleep, her dreams swirled. She was trapped in a dark hole or closet somewhere strange, in some place she didn't know, and a man who resembled Sacha Bernard was laughing at her and taunting her. It was as if she could not move.

"Wake up, Luz!" Someone was calling her name and shaking her. "Luz! Luz, wake up!"

She opened her eyes. It was Sara, a look of concern on her face.

"Here, drink some water. You are sweating like crazy. When I unlocked the door and came into the room, you were writhing around in the bed like you were sleeping in an anthill." Sara felt Luz's forehead. "You feel cool, so you must not have a fever."

Luz gulped the water down and sat up in bed. She blinked a few times and wiped the sandy goop out of her eyes.

"That was some dream. I feel like I was asleep forever. What time is it?"

"Five-thirty."

While they were getting ready for dinner, Luz and Sara shared the details of their day's events. Sara was thrilled by the reception she had received at the winery when she stopped by on her way to Sonoma. So many of the staff expressed their condolences about her grandfather and offered to help her in any way they could.

Sara told Luz that when she first unlocked her grandfather's office, she was so overcome by memories of him that she didn't even notice there was a letter addressed to Orval from Paul Angel on the top of her grandfather's desk.

"I really didn't know what to do. I just stared at it for a few minutes, then realized someone had to open it and it might as well be me," Sara said to Luz, who was listening attentively as put on her lip gloss.

"The letter said he would be away for a week or so and to refer any questions to Fred Bowman, the assistant winemaker who I've never met."

While she pulled on her jeans, Luz said, "I'm so surprised that Paul Angel left at the beginning of the harvest. Isn't that one of the most important times in the growing season?"

"Yes, it's crucial to the outcome of the wine. Maybe he really did poison grandpa and left to avoid arrest. I never thought I would be living through this nightmare, "Sara said, exasperated.

"No one thought your grandfather would die this way,"Luz blurted out.

"And if this assistant winemaker is taking care of day-to-day management, then who is making the wine?" Sara asked.

Luz tried to calm her. "Sacha and I will be working on various things over this important weekend, Sara, and we want you to have the best possible introduction to the valley, and to stay safe and out of trouble. Keep your eyes open and let me know if you hear or see or experience anything odd. And please don't tell anyone I shared all this with you. "

"And why not? What are you going to be working on with Sacha that you can't tell me about? It will be my winery in a few years!" Sara looked indignant.

"Yes, I know it's your winery, but in this case you already know something isn't right. Like the assistant winemaker acting like he knows what he is doing: it's obvious he's clueless about the wine business. There is something weird about this entire situation. By the way, do you have the note from Paul Angel?"

"Yes, I brought it here to show it to Sacha, my aunt and to you. Here it is," Sara said, as she handed Luz an ecru envelope, that Luz delicately handled with a Kleenex, wrapping it up, stowing it in the room safe.

"It needs to be checked for fingerprints and the signature compared with that of the codicil. Martin Cohen will help us get this to the right people so we can figure out what is going on at Chateau La Mer," Luz said.

"Above all, Sara, we want you safe, so follow your schedule and don't go anywhere alone for the next few days. Make sure you are always in a big group, and figure out who your friends are here. That is all I am going to tell you now. OK?" Luz spoke

like she was Sara's big sister—firmly, yet with a touch of softness.

"We don't want anything to happen to you," she continued.
"Sacha is very concerned, too. Both of you could be in serious
danger."

Sara nodded, and tears started down her cheeks. Luz came
over to give her a hug, and the two sat on the bed together as
Sara poured out her heart to her.

"This was supposed to be a weekend with my grandfather, my introduction to the wine community. I was looking
forward to it so much. I know I am still in college, and I'm not
really ready to take over, but this is my heritage, this is my
future, and now it is such a mess, and so sad at the same time."

Luz handed her a tissue. "I know you miss your Grandfather Orval. And probably your parents too. Just like a string of
pearls, these losses connect together. You are a strong person,
Sara, and you will get through this weekend, and this loss. You
have a whole team of people on your side, and this mess will
get straightened out sooner than you think."

Luz and Sara donned comfortable shoes and warm sweat-
ers, since they were meeting Clint and Michelle at the local
Bistro Grill, just a few blocks away. Sara made an effort to be
cheerful, asking, "Are you looking forward to seeing Jeff tomorrow at the track?"

Luz looked at her and smiled. "Nothing makes me happier
than to be with him. And he is happiest at the track. He is in
his element."

Sara smiled wistfully. "I wish I could find someone like that.
I intimidate so many guys, or rather my future with Chateau

La Mer does. The professors in my oenology and viticulture classes keep reminding them that I am not just an ordinary girl."

"I didn't expect to meet someone like Jeff in my day-to-day life," Luz said. "Clint and Michelle gave us a chance to meet. You'll find the right guy for you when it's the right time. And you want someone who will look out for your best interests over his own, which is hard to find."

"Jeff seems perfect to me," Sara said. "And he looks dreamy in his tuxedo."

"Yes, he does. But he is not one for the party scene. I am lucky he is arriving in time for the *Nuit Blanche* dinner, which he's promised me he'll go to even though he is not thrilled about it. It should be great people watching!"

The two women continued chatting as they left the hotel and found their way to the small bistro.

CHAPTER 11

At a restaurant up the road from Napa, in Oakville, Roger Schneider sat at a quiet corner table waiting for his guests to arrive. Girard Morel and his girlfriend, Giselle Mouton, were joining him to meet with Sacha Bernard.

Roger had great hopes he could convince Sacha Bernard to give him and his driver Matt Locke a chance at a Formula International test in Europe after the Sonoma race. It was known that the Chateau Bernard race team was looking for new talent, and that new talent would have to pass a test.

Any driver who was not yet in the series had to demonstrate their skills by driving a car that was designed and set up to comply with the specifications stipulated by the Formula International Racing series. Depending on the average lap times around the track and the condition of the car, tires, and suspension after the test, a driver might or might not qualify to move up to Formula International as a full-time driver with a ride paid for by sponsors and team owners.

To move up to the prestigious racing series that traveled all over the globe would be the crown in Matt Locke's racing career, giving Schneider access to billions of dollars in sponsorship and connections he could parlay into even more money.

Looking up from his phone, Roger saw Morel walking to the table and greeted him. "Hey, Girard, ready for tonight?"

"Yes, my friend. I'm looking forward to capturing the interest of this famous Frenchman. And of course if I'm not able to do so, then the lovely Giselle will do it for me," Morel answered.

"And where is your lovely lady?" Roger asked, looking toward the door.

"She stopped for a selfie with one of the local winemakers. I believe she is planning to ambush Sacha Bernard when he drives up to valet parking," Morel chuckled. "First a photo, then she will place her arm in his, and then he will offer to buy her a drink, and she will walk him to our table. Simple."

"I talked to Mauricio yesterday. He's got a few accounts set up for us offshore, if we need them," Roger said.

"That man charges a fortune to provide that service, Roger. You really need to find a better way to deal with your funds. I'm afraid one of these days Mauricio is going to pay you back for the trouble you caused him at Indianapolis."

"We're old friends," Roger said. "He knows about my skeletons and I know about his. We'll be fine. Don't worry about it."

Roger had met Girard Morel through Luz Maria Dane's old boyfriend, Mauricio, when Mauricio set up a money-laundering scheme to fund Roger and the Blackbird Racing Team.

Morel originally ran a bucket shop specializing in small penny stocks, then decided to branch out to do initial public offerings of some very new Silicon Valley companies. During that time, he sold shares in a few of those to Roger, who luckily struck it rich on one that was bought out for billions just in the last year, more than two years after it went public. When the price of those shares skyrocketed, Roger became a multimillionaire and suddenly had the money to make his team more competitive in the racing series.

"Matt Locke looks and acts like an entirely different guy since Giselle started working with him," Roger said.

"She is a tough media trainer. First she takes all those photos and videos and makes you look at them, and then off you go to buy new clothes, new hairstyles, and facials. I hope she doesn't convince him to wear makeup."

"Makeup!?" Roger said, raising his eyebrows. Then he smiled. "Here is the beautiful lady now, and as you predicted, she is arm-in-arm with Sacha Bernard."

Giselle walked up with Sacha by her side. Her beige leather miniskirt accentuated the tan of her shapely legs, while the tight brown, beige, and black polka-dot T-shirt showed off her other assets. She smiled seductively as she smoothed her skirt to sit down at the table.

Roger had met Giselle Mouton through hobnobbing with Girard Morel. Giselle, a Parisian social media star and tabloid reporter, served as a prospector for Morel, finding him new clients. As a favor to Roger, Giselle worked with Matt Locke on his social media platforms, interviewing skills, and total presentation, to make him a more appealing prospect for the

FIR series.

Giselle, a tall, leggy former model, was always seen by Matt's side, setting up photo shoots and interviews with other international media sites that could increase the value of his brand around the world. When she wasn't with Matt, Giselle would search out the wealthiest sponsors or fans at whatever event they attended, then introduce them to Morel as potential investors in his venture capital fund. With his success with the technology companies Clambake© and Trade2©, he advertised that he had a waiting list of interested investors and made an effort to pick and choose whose money he wanted to invest.

"Bonsoir," Sacha greeted everyone, then seated himself across from Giselle, next to Roger. He did not feel the need to introduce himself to Roger or Girard, since he already knew them by reputation.

Sacha was a regular at this restaurant, so the waiter instantly appeared with his favorite sparkling wine, L'Étoile du Mer, four glasses, and a special filtered ashtray that would keep the smoke from his Gitanes from disturbing the other patrons. A plate of pate, gherkins, crudités, and sliced bread appeared immediately afterward.

"Such an intimate dinner party," Sacha said. "Or is this a business meeting?"

Girard and Roger spoke over each other, one saying, "A casual dinner, of course," and the other, "Yes, we'd like to discuss business."

"Ah, I see," Sacha said, lighting up one of his cigarettes after offering them to the others at the table, with no takers.

"I do not care to discuss business before, during or after dinner. Since I did not tell you that before I accepted your invitation, I will keep this to a short visit, and then go on my way. Tell me, what do you want?" Sacha said firmly.

"Oh, Sacha, surely you don't mean that you don't want to have dinner with me tonight?" Giselle asked in her sensual purr.

"Giselle, I have known you for many years. Do not think you can use your beauty to lead me to believe you are interested in me for personal reasons, when we both know you are really only interested in my business assets."

Girard looked over at Roger, and when he realized Sacha had called for the check, he decided to cut to the chase. "I want to buy your company."

"Very direct. I like that in a conversation about business," Sacha said, "but my answer is no. Chateau La Mer and Chateau Bernard are not for sale."

"But your partners, they may not feel that way," Girard replied.

"One of my partners, one of my best friends, died last week. I know he never wanted to sell his shares in the company. And my other partner, Paul Angel, has spent his life making the best wine in the world, so I believe he feels the same way." Sacha's voice started out low and steadily grew louder.

"I have spoken with Paul Angel, and he said that he's interested in selling and that he controls at least half of the company now that Orval Slattery is dead. So maybe you should rethink your position, Mr. Bernard," said Morel, his tone curt and precise.

Sacha lit another cigarette and took another sip of the champagne. He looked at Roger, Girard, and Giselle and nodded.

"I see. So you plan to buy my company. Will you take it public, which is your specialty, Girard, if I may call you Girard, and in the process double your money? Or will you sell it privately by starting a bidding war for my company and sell it to one of the many conglomerates that already has a portfolio of small boutique wineries around the world?" Sacha asked, his voice low and menacing.

Morel stared at him, then shifted his gaze to the bubbles in his champagne flute.

"Since there are four of you in on this, what will you each make on this deal, in addition to the profit from the ultimate sale of my company? And yes, I mean four of you. The Paul Angel I know will never sell his company. You will have to kill him to get control of it. And kill me too," Sacha said. He signed the check, stood up from the table, and walked out the door.

Girard Morel looked at Giselle and Roger and said, "*Merde!*"

CHAPTER 12

The morning dawned cold and gray, the mist from the ocean moving across the valley to the hills where rows and rows of vines sagged with grapes ready for the harvest. Slow-moving farm trucks were hauling beds of just-picked fruit to wineries all over the Sonoma Valley. Interspersed with the old agricultural equipment that wound up and down the narrow roads were sleek transport trailers emblazoned with advertisements for pharmaceuticals, breakfast foods, and motor oil. On the way to the Sonoma raceway, once known as Sears Point Raceway, were the Indy car haulers loaded with 200 mph race cars, the fastest vehicles of the North American racing circuit.

Arriving at the raceway, Jeff Harwood checked in with the credentials office, collected the passes for his sponsors for the weekend and the schedule for his crew and drivers, and received instructions on where to park the transporter and where to set up the team garage for the weekend. Weary after the drive from Texas, Jeff nodded repetitively at the track official speaking to him, hoping he would remember what he was being told so he wouldn't have to come back for further instructions. Without Luz to take care of the details, Jeff noticed he was often late for meetings, lost at the new speedways, and frequently missing a decal or patch necessary for the collection of the prize money he sorely wanted and needed. It wasn't the same without her.

Listlessly walking back to the big semi, Jeff was jolted out of his funk by the honking of an ice-blue Mustang convertible speeding toward him. It stopped right in front of the hauler. The driver wore a cream-colored Stetson, and shimmering auburn hair peeked out from under a pink scarf wrapped around the passenger's head. A glimmer of recognition arose on Jeff's face, then he burst into a big smile, walked over to the car, pulled the door open, and leaned in to give the willowy redhead a warm hug. "Michelle! I have never been so glad to see two people in my whole life. It was a long drive from San Antonio."

Jeff then walked around to the driver's side and shook Clint Amberson's hand.

"How is my favorite partner doing? I like your ride. What year is this?" Jeff asked, looking over the classic Mustang convertible.

"I'll tell you once we get it parked in the right place. Where are we working this weekend? They told me I could park nearby so I wouldn't have to walk too far," Clint said, gesturing toward his cane.

Jeff motioned for Clint and the semi driver to follow him,

then led them to the garages lined up between the last turn on the road course and the front straight. Once they found their assigned garage space, they could park the trailer right in front of it, unload the cars, the toolboxes, and set up tables and chairs for sponsors and team members. Jeff motioned for Clint to park right behind the semi, where there was space for one car. While the team saw to the tools and equipment, Jeff set up a small café table with matching folding chairs right inside the garage for Clint and Michelle Amberson.

While in his early twenties, Jeff had worked as a roustabout for Clint's oil company and later was a grunt on his team the first year Clint fielded a car for the Indy 500. Earlier this year, when Jeff's car was destroyed right before it qualified at Indy, and Clint's crew chief and team manager quit only moments before the race began, Clint and Jeff formed a new team known as Amberson-Harwood Racing, all because Luz Dane had insisted it was a brilliant solution to problems both teams had to resolve in order to compete at the 500-mile race.

It had been a long summer for Jeff: he had gone from Indianapolis to Loudon, Kansas City, Las Vegas, Fort Worth, and now Sonoma. He had made it back to the shop in Boerne, Texas, once or twice, most recently the weekend before, to attend the gala where Orval Slattery had been murdered. All summer he'd been representing the team ownership at all the tracks: Clint was still in rehab following the stroke that had paralyzed him a month before the Indianapolis 500. Jeff entertained sponsor representatives and employees, made countless personal appearances, and posed for thousands of photographs, with rarely a moment's break or any time on his own.

He and Clint stayed in touch by phone and email, going over budget figures and sponsor requests long-distance, doing everything necessary to get funding for the next season that began in March. It had been so long since Clint and Michelle had joined him at a racetrack that if he hadn't seen the cowboy hat and the auburn hair, he wouldn't have believed it was them.

Seated at the table, sipping coffee, Jeff sighed gratefully at the sight of his two friends. Clint was now walking with the help of a cane and seemed more alert and interested in the mechanical goings-on around him in the garage area. Michelle looked over at Jeff, her green eyes filled with mischief, and in her best sugarcoated drawl said, "Honey, you look a little tired, and a little bit, hmmm, lonely. Is that right?"

Jeff looked at her and tipped his chair back on two legs. "Yes, it would have helped to have Luz along on my trip out here, but some friend gave her the idea she should start her own business, and so she decided to do that and for the last three months she's been busy transferring her accounts, signing up clients, and battling with that firm where she used to work. She tells me it will give her more independence once she has everything done, but I haven't seen any evidence of that as of yet. I know she was on the plane with you two coming out here, but she is all wrapped up with that Chateau La Mer business, helping your niece stay out of jail and hold on to the business her grandfather left her. When she shows up, I'll know she's here."

Clint chuckled as he watched Jeff talk to Michelle as if he

didn't realize the part she played in the new life of Luz Dane. Michelle smiled like a Cheshire cat, knowing that Luz and Sara were about thirty minutes behind them on the highway, following two days of work regarding Chateau La Mer. Most likely they were now at the credentials office and would drive up shortly to join them at the garage area.

"Lookin' over this-here schedule, it sure seems mighty highfalutin here in Sonoma. It says there is a celebrity wine tasting and Calcutta that benefits local charities, something called 'Nut Blank' and just a little bit o' racing," Clint said as he read through the events for the next three days. "Seems like a lot of stuff to fit into one weekend."

"Oh, sweetheart, that is *Nuit Blanche*, French for White Night. Everyone wears white. You know it will be fun," Michelle said, squeezing his arm. "Besides, Sacha will be here. It's been years since we've all been together at a racetrack, and he is so interesting. I wonder which royal family spent the summer at his chateau this year? Speaking of chateaus, here's Miss Chateau La Mer herself. Hi, Sara!"

Michelle waved as she got up from the table to greet Sara, then turned to Jeff. "My goodness, look who's here. Is that Luz?"

Jeff stood by as Michelle greeted both the girls with hugs and the perfunctory air kisses. Clint watched him carefully as the women fussed over each other, then said, "She is one good-lookin' filly. Be careful with her, son. She might get away from you if you aren't careful. I know what I'm talking about. It almost happened to me—I almost lost Michelle to another."

Jeff raised his left eyebrow at Clint, then stepped forward

and took Luz in his arms. He gave her a strong hug and kissed her on the lips.

"I'm glad you're back. I've missed you not being around at the races since Indianapolis. Things just don't work right. It's not the same without you by my side," Jeff said.

Luz smiled. Jeff's confession that he missed her was very touching. It was something she always hoped to hear from him. But his chaste hug and kiss were less passionate than she had expected: when she last saw him, they couldn't seem to keep away from each other.

While Luz was thinking about what she wanted to say to him, another vehicle drove up, this one a Bentley convertible with a mustachioed driver at the helm smoking a cigarette and talking on his phone. As he approached the crowd, he locked up the brakes, and spun the car around so the driver's-side door was right next to Michelle. The six-foot, four-inch driver stepped out of the car and swept Michelle off her feet, cradling her in his arms and kissing her squarely on the lips. Then he said, with a French accent, "Nothing has changed! You, Michelle, are still the most delicious woman I have ever known. Clint, you lucky dog, to have a wife like her, so beautiful and so luscious. How are you, old man?"

Sacha Bernard had arrived at the track with a flourish and in grand style. He shook hands with all the men, gave hugs to all the women, and seemed to be everywhere, looking at everything, all at one time. Luz had never seen a more energetic man. He oozed charm and grace, yet also exuded strength and machismo; his physique rivaled that of any other man at the track. Luz wondered what his history was with Michelle: it was the second time she had seen an annoyed look on Clint's face as he watched her be swept away by the Frenchman.

Sacha then exclaimed, "Ah, Sara. I am sorry I missed you this morning at the winery. I will be eager to hear what you learned today."

Jeff stood by, watching Sacha charm all the women around him. Clint, too, was aware of the Frenchman's magical effect on the group.

"Remember, Jeff, you've got to race your own race, not somebody else's. Time to get to work. You've got to get your drivers qualified tomorrow, and today is the only day for practice before the race. Don't worry about Michelle and me, we'll be fine. I've got my hands full keeping her away from that Frenchman, but you can count on us for every meal and all the festivities," Clint said as he ambled over to the garage area, leaning on his cane.

Michelle saw him walking away from the group and knew she'd better follow. Clint was so stubborn he was liable to end up in one of the race cars on the track if she wasn't watching him. She grabbed her bag, air-kissed the girls, and gave Sacha a peck on the cheek, then quickly caught up to Clint, linking her arm in his.

Jeff was directing as the crewmembers began popping out of the hauler and the motor home to set up the assigned pit box with their equipment and unfurl the awning that would serve as the team's hospitality tent. More chairs and tables were unloaded and arranged, and a public address system and speakers were produced from the rear-loading bay. Parked side by side, the hauler and motor home created a small compound where the awnings protruded like wings from the two vehicles; the motor home awning would be used for entertainment, and the hauler's awning would serve as a hospitality area. Each mechanic unloaded his rolling toolbox and placed it in the perimeter of the garage space. One end backed up to the garage, leaving about fifty feet between the hauler and the garage door opening, giving pit carts room to tow the cars in and out of the garages. It was similar to Indy in that each team had an enclosed garage where they could secure their cars and tools, yet they had to cover some distance to get to the pit roads and the track.

With only Sara and Luz to entertain him, Sacha watched with fascination as the crew performed their maneuvers setting up the garage and pit box. Practiced and proud of their work, Jeff's team walked through their carefully choreographed routine undistracted by the social goings-on around them. When they were finally finished, they lowered the lift carrying one of the chassis and unloaded the Indy car to be driven by Christi Cole, then repeated that process for the car Mark Miller would drive. Another transporter waited for them in the outer parking lot filled with two more cars, extra parts and wheels, special tools, and surplus equipment. Jeff hoped he wouldn't need all the extras, but he wanted them available just in case.

One by one the cars were towed to the fueling station and then back to the pit box. The scoring stand was already in place; monitors were connected to the ports accessing the on-time track data. Tires were stacked up, easily accessible when the time came to switch out the sets. An ice chest held cold drinks for the crew and drivers.

"Very nice. Very nice," Sacha said to Jeff as he watched the younger man check that all the equipment was placed where it belonged. "I am so impressed by how it is all organized. How everything has a place. How your men know where to put everything. I have only seen this kind of organization from a Formula International team. I know why Clint relies on you, Jeff," Sacha said pronouncing Jeff with a very soft *J* sound. "You must come to Europe for one of the races. Who knows, maybe you will have your own FIR team someday."

He lit a cigarette, offering one to Jeff too. Although Jeff would have preferred one of his own cigarettes, he accepted the one Sacha offered, not wanting to offend the emphatic Frenchman. The strong Gitanes surprised him, but he enjoyed the different taste experience.

While the two men discussed the nuances of open-wheel racing in America and abroad, Christi Cole joined Sara and Luz, who were enmeshed in a serious conversation about Orval Slattery's estate. Wearing her red and white driving suit, Christi looked fresh and eager after her trip to Sonoma aboard the team motor coach that she and Mark Miller called home during the season. Luz looked up from the notes she was making on a legal pad, saw Christi, and jumped up to give her a big hug, then introduced her to Sara. Embroidered on the right-hand side of her driving suit was the small VS logo of one of Christi's sponsors. When Luz saw it, she laughed. "It is so good to see you. I told you that company would give you a sponsorship deal."

The two women laughed, remembering the first time Luz

had brought up the international lingerie company as a potential sponsor for Christi.

"After all, you are the fastest woman in racing. You've had an incredible season—two podium finishes, not counting the wins at Loudon or Indy. I am so glad you saved this team when we asked you to drive for us at the speedway."

"Hey, Christi, there is someone here I'd like to introduce you to," Jeff called out when he noticed she was dressed and ready for practice.

Her short platinum-blonde hair accentuating her elfin good looks, Christi smiled as she turned toward Jeff. Luz thought the two exchanged a look that seemed like more than a "boss and subordinate" look, but it lingered for just a moment and then was gone.

Jeff said, "Christi, I want you to meet Sacha Bernard. He owns a Formula International team and is a partner in Chateau La Mer with Sara Slattery, who you just met. He and Clint and Michelle have been friends for years. Maybe he'll give you that chance you've been hoping for to make it onto the international circuit."

Sacha stood up and walked forward to meet Christi, then he bowed down toward her petite frame, took her hand gently in his, and kissed it softly. He focused his soulful brown-gold eyes on her and said, "It is my pleasure to meet such a beautiful creature. You are like a little doll, a little racing doll. Surely you want to come to Europe and drive in the FIR series, *n'est-ce pas*? It is where all the great drivers want to be. We will see how you do this weekend and then maybe you can come to see me for, for, what do they call it, for a test ride?"

"Mr. Bernard, it is such an honor to meet you. Thank you for the offer, but I already have a ride. And even if I did want to try Formula International, I couldn't go without Jeff. He's really helped me get to where I am now, so I couldn't just leave him or his team. You understand that kind of loyalty, don't you?" Christi said, gazing at Jeff.

Jeff smiled back at her. Luz wondered what was going on. Most drivers would jump at a chance to drive for a FIR team. What had been going on between Jeff and Christi while Luz was setting up her business? Was Jeff falling for Christi? Or was Christi helping Jeff with his own career? Luz didn't know what to think, but she intended to find out more over the weekend.

CHAPTER 13

Entering the Sonoma Gardens, where tiny fairy lights illuminated the trees and billowing white tents covered the grand courtyard, Luz caught her breath at the beauty of the *Nuit Blanche* setting. All of the guests were wearing white, and the tables were set with silver flatware, elaborate candelabras, and glittering crystal stemware.

When Sacha Bernard invited the wine community and other luminaries to an event, he wanted it to feel like it was taking place in Paris, in the Tuileries. Every guest was handed a glass of sparkling wine, a program of the evening's events, and their table assignment. Sara was to be seated at the head table, with Sacha as her escort in lieu of her late grandfather, Orval Slattery. Michelle and Clint were also seated there in deference to the racing community's role in the coming weekend's events.

Luz and Jeff wandered around the gardens to look at the

various offerings for the evening's auction. Items donated for bidding included cases of wine from the top five vineyards, and private dinners or lunches with tours of those wineries. The grand prize—a trip to the FIR race in Monaco, hosted by Sacha Bernard, followed by a trip to his French wine properties between Lyon and Dijon—was of great interest to everyone.

When it was time to be seated, Luz caught Sara's eye and pointed at the microphone, prompting Sara to stand up, turn the mike on, and say in a soft, sultry voice, "Welcome! So glad all of you could join us tonight! It should be an exciting evening."

The crowd clapped and laughed.

Sara continued, "We are all so lucky to be enjoying the hospitality of one of the world's most celebrated industrialists, Sacha Bernard. He needs no further introduction, so Sacha, thank you for being our host this evening." She passed him the microphone as he rose.

Sacha shared the plan for the evening: after dinner, there would be music for dancing, followed by the auction and then dessert. He listed the wine pairings that would make this meal one of the most memorable for those lucky enough to enjoy it, and quickly described the FIR jaunt to encourage more bidding at auction time. Then he sat down at Sara's right side.

Seated at the table with Luz and Jeff was the founder of GMB Financial, Girard Morel, who ran a financial services firm specializing in start-ups and penny stocks. He had become a billionaire when one of his penny stock deals turned into the darling of a well-known Silicon Valley venture capital firm. With his windfall came notoriety and cultivated expensive taste, including fast cars, award-winning wines, and beautiful women, one of whom was on his arm for the *Nuit Blanche* event.

"Let me introduce you to Giselle Mouton," Girard said to Luz and Jeff when they approached the table. The four exchanged pleasantries, and before they sat down at the table, Giselle quickly rearranged the place cards so she was seated next to Jeff, while Girard sat next to Luz.

Luz asked Girard about his interests. He answered, "I help companies go from private ownership to public offerings, successfully."

Luz was intrigued but confused. "Do you have a card? I'd like to be able to contact you later in case I want to know more."

They exchanged cards, and while she glanced at the expensive card stock and stroked her thumb over the engraving of the GMB logo, she vaguely recalled something about a GMB financial company being just a glorified bucket shop, buying and selling stocks over and over creating a market that ultimately left some investors holding the bag of a high-priced security that they could only liquidate at a loss.

Luz wondered why he was attending the *Nuit Blanche* event. Was he prospecting future clients? Did he have connections in the valley?

"That must be interesting work," Luz said, hoping to open the door to more conversation.

"Yes, I am working on the deal of a lifetime that I hope will come to fruition. In fact, a friend of mine, Paul, is very interested in the possibility of taking his company public," Girard said. Then, momentarily distracted, he got up from the table abruptly and disappeared into the crowd.

Giselle, watching Girard, also rose from the table and, after excusing herself, followed him into the darkness.

While Giselle had prattled on about her job with the French tabloid '*Qu'est que se?*' Jeff had noticed the whispering back and forth between Luz and Girard. Why had Giselle rearranged the place cards so Luz sat next to her date? All Giselle talked about was herself and all the open-wheel races she'd attended all over the world. When he tried to converse with her, she would ignore him and instead inquire about some celebrity seated at another table nearby.

When she and Girard left, Jeff scooted over to his original seat next to Luz, put the place cards in their original spots, and just focused on the plates before him and the wine that went with them, hoping to add a bit of culture to his base of knowledge.

Luz smiled and kissed him on the cheek. "Thank goodness we're back together. I missed you."

She raised her glass to him and they toasted the evening together. Picking up her knife and fork and saying, "This looks delicious," Luz started on her entrée.

After the main course, paired with three different Chateau La Mer cabernet sauvignon wines, from the last three vintage years, Jeff noticed how Luz was looking at the head table, trying to make eye contact with Sacha or Sara, and then popping up from her seat, only to sit down again, when another person appeared to occupy the two hosts' attention. Since both were effectively hosting the event, it would be difficult to get them alone, out of earshot of anyone.

"Your only chance to talk with either of them will be after this shindig, Luz. The band has started up, so let's dance." Jeff stood up and offered her his hand.

Luz happily took his arm, and he held her close as they danced to a romantic ballad that segued into a swing beat, leading Jeff to twirl her around the dance floor. Just as the second song ended, Sacha Bernard and Sara came dancing up to them, and Sacha suggested they change partners. Jeff was a little miffed but said, "OK. I think Luz wants to talk with you, anyway."

The minute they started to dance, the band began a loud rock-and-roll cover of a popular ballad, making it hard for Sacha and Luz to talk to one another. He made several attempts to turn it into a swing dance as Luz tried to tell him all about her cryptic conversation with Girard Morel, and his reference to a friend wanting to take a company public.

When the music stopped, Sacha said, "I do not want to talk about this anymore during my party. We will talk later, Luz."

Politely clapping for the band, Sacha handed Luz back to Jeff and offered Sara his arm so they could return to the head table. With the auction about to begin, the band played a brass clarion call and asked that all guests return to their seats at their assigned tables.

On returning to their table, Jeff and Luz were surprised to see that Clint and Michelle had joined them.

"Can't bid on anything if I'm seated at that head table," Clint said.

Bidding with enthusiasm, guests quickly snapped up the

wines from the five major vineyards. Michelle managed to purchase the most highly rated of the wines when her competition was distracted by the waiter pouring wine at his table.

Luz was carefully observing who was seated where and with whom. Sacha was moving among the tables complimenting both those who bought wine and those who bid but lost. Sara was working the other side of the gardens, thanking those people who hadn't bid yet for attending and making the charity event a grand success. With an enthusiastic smile she reminded them of the fabulous opportunity to bid on the Formula International trek and winery tour, which hopefully would be the big money maker of the evening. Sara's warm personality was evident as she played the perfect hostess for the special evening.

With a rumbling drum roll that heralded the auctioning of the fantastic trip to the French Chateau Bernard winery and vineyards along with luxurious accommodations, pit road seating, and parties at the Monaco Grand Prix race, all heads turned to the bandstand, where Sacha Bernard described the fabulous opportunity that awaited the highest bidder. Once he turned it over to the auctioneer, guests quickly started raising their paddles to bid on the luxurious trip.

Knowing she did not have the means to compete with the various Silicon Valley billionaires or the celebrities and professional athletes in attendance, Luz watched in awe as the price for the trip soared in the first few moments of the auction.

Their tablemate, Girard Morel, along with his girlfriend, Giselle, had returned to their seats. He held his paddle in his hand while his arm moved up and down like a jack-in-the-box, constantly popping up each time another bid beat his. After a few minutes there were only two bidders: Morel and one man standing in the shadows of the fairy lights.

When the price was over a million dollars, the auctioneer insisted that the hidden guest come forward so his paddle would be more visible. As his face was illuminated and Luz saw who it was, she gasped.

"It's Roger Schneider. Where did he get this kind of money?" Luz said in a whisper loud enough for Michelle and Jeff to hear.

At last Morel graciously gave in, announcing that he would allow the man in the corner of the garden to win the auction bid. The crowd applauded the competition, and the auctioneer echoed their sentiments, announcing that it had been a fast-paced race to the win for the Grand Prix trip and that the Children's Charities of Sonoma appreciated the generosity of Mr. Roger Schneider and Blackbird Racing.

Girard Morel went over to congratulate Schneider. Their conversation lasted several minutes, and when he returned to the table for dessert, he was beaming.

"That fellow Schneider is such a nice guy. When I went over to congratulate him, he offered to sell me the trip for just a hundred grand over what he paid for it. I'll even get the deduction for his bid amount if I pay for it tonight! He invited me to watch the race this weekend from the Blackbird pits. Wow!"

Luz, Clint, Michelle, and Jeff all stared at Morel, not believing what they were hearing. They were appalled, understanding that Schneider had just bid up the trip for the publicity and was now making a cool hundred grand for playing Morel as a sucker.

Not wanting to shut down his enthusiasm or do irreparable damage to what could be a helpful friendship, Luz did her best to offer sincere congratulations. "Fantastic! You are going to have the best time. Lucky for you Schneider was so willing to give up this chance that will never come along again."

"Oh, he assured me there will be another chance for him. I've known Roger for a few years. He invested in one of my penny stocks, the same one that became an overnight sensation and a darling of Wall Street. That's where most of his money comes from, and sponsorships too, of course. He's got some in with the winery—knows Paul, one of the partners. They are great friends, apparently. That's why I'll be in his pits. They have a deal of some sort."

"Well, I'm sure you'll have the time of your life, this weekend and in France. So great to hear of your good luck!" Luz said, shaking his hand.

Clint, Michelle, and Jeff were stunned by what they heard, and Clint looked like he was ready to start a ruckus, but Michelle suddenly realized that Luz was working to pull as much information as she could from this man, information that could help Sara and Sacha. Michelle gave her husband a quick kiss and rubbed his shoulder tenderly, doing her best to soothe him. Jeff was still miffed by the attention Luz was giving this billionaire, but Michelle raised her eyebrows at him and mouthed, "I can explain."

Jeff looked at Michelle crossly. "I've had about as much fun here as I can. I think it is time to get some shut-eye, if I can get my date's attention so I can escort her back to the hotel."

"Wait, Jeff. The band is starting up again. Why don't you and Luz have another glass of champagne, and dance for a couple of songs. It really is romantic here, and you both have a lot of work ahead of you. I think you've been away from each other too long. Please, for me," Michelle pleaded.

Luz turned around and heard the band playing one of her favorite songs, "*La Vie en Rose*." She gently kissed Jeff on the cheek and asked him to dance.

His green eyes softened. Hand in hand they walked out to the dance floor, where he tenderly took her in his arms for a graceful dance.

BARBIE O'CONNOR

CHAPTER 14

Both Sara and Luz were up early, Sara to head off to the winery, and Luz to the track for final practice and qualifying. Sipping a cup of coffee in their room while Sara applied mascara, Luz asked, "Would your grandfather have kept any photo albums where Paul Angel might be pictured? Maybe something with news clippings when the winery first opened, or maybe after the French/American wine challenge when Chateau La Mer surprised the judges?"

"Hmmm, there is that one picture. I thought you saw it, the one at his house, with the three men. My grandfather was in his army uniform, and Sacha and Paul were by his side. There might be some here, some kind of archives. He kept an extensive library of books on oenology, viticulture, terroir, and art as it related to wine," Sara said as she brushed her wavy auburn hair and put on gold hoop earrings. "I can look when I am there today, if it would help you."

"Sara, I would rather have a look at those archives myself. I am afraid someone might get concerned about your interest in the history of Chateau La Mer and try to harm you. Right now we don't want people at the winery to find you threatening in any way."

"Luz, you keep talking about keeping me safe and out of harm's way. Is my life really in danger?" Sara looked Luz's reflection in the mirror.

"Sara, I'm afraid your grandfather's murder is part of a plan to take over Chateau La Mer. The new codicil that Martin Cohen received naming Paul Angel as the trustee, instead of you, puts him in control of half of the shares of the company. In Sacha's estate planning, as I understand it, he left his shares in trust going to you, as long as you live past your twenty-fifth birthday," Luz stated.

"But if I die before I'm twenty-five, what happens to those shares?" Sara asked, her eyes wide.

"Sacha said they go in trust to the employees of the winery, and whoever is running the winery will be the trustee of that trust."

"So if I die, and Sacha dies, then Paul Angel controls a majority of shares. And can do whatever he wants to with the winery." Sara stared out into space.

"Yes. And when I was conversing with Girard Morel last night, I heard him mention some big deal that he is putting together with his friend Paul. Maybe it's some other Paul, but I don't think so."

"I never met Paul Angel. But he was the one who packed the wine for my grandfather's trip to Texas, where he died.

Where he was poisoned."

"Yes, and he is trustee of your trust now. Only Orval and Sacha really knew him or could identify him. There are no pictures of him on social media prior to last night. According to Sacha, he was very reclusive and wanted Orval and Sacha to be the front men for the winery. So that is why I want to look in the archives—to see if I can find anything that would help us identify him."

"OK, I will watch out for myself. When can you meet me at the winery?" Sara asked.

"Qualifying ends at three this afternoon. How about I meet you afterwards? It will take me about thirty to forty-five minutes to get there."

"That would work. I don't have another event until seven this evening, so there should be time for you to at least get started looking through the library."

"Good, I'll see you there," Luz said as she picked up her bag and started out the door. Suddenly she stopped and walked back into the room and looked directly at Sara.

"Please don't sign any documents or checks over the next few days, even if someone insists. Just say you need time to carefully read them, or change the subject. Whatever excuse you give, try to get them in your hands and then bring them to me, please, so I can look them over and if necessary, get them to Sacha or Martin Cohen."

"Actually, there were a bunch of papers on Grandfather Orval's desk with a note attached saying my signature was needed on them," Sara said. "Luckily, I got a phone call just as I started to look at them, and then had to leave for an appointment. I assume they are still on the desk waiting for me."

"Bring them back here tonight in this portfolio. I want to read them and then maybe have someone examine them. There is something weird going on with this Paul Angel situation, and I can't put my finger on it," Luz said. "Please be careful, Sara. I suspect that there are some powerful people literally banking on Chateau La Mer to make all their dreams come true."

Luz handed her the portfolio she used for client documents, a leather envelope clutch embossed with her initials, having emptied it while they were talking.

Looking at her watch, she grabbed her keys and backpack, hugged Sara, and walked out the door. Texting that she was on her way to the track, Luz almost bumped into Girard Morel as he walked down the hallway toward her room.

"Pardon me," Luz said, looking up from her phone. "Oh, Girard, I didn't know you were staying here too. You disappeared last night after dessert, and I assumed you left before we did."

"Luz—that's your name, right? Well, I'd planned to go back to Mountview, but there are a few details I am trying to wrap up on this new public offering. Wire transfer authorizations, that kind of thing. I'm sure you know what is required, since you are in the business." Girard smiled.

"Yes, but I've never been on the ground floor of taking a company public," Luz said coyly, longingly.

"When I'm done with this deal, I'll tell you all about it," Girard said. "It's confidential, you know. Any leaks and the deal could fall apart. I'm sure you understand."

"Yes, I do," Luz said, sighing.

"Maybe I can give you an overview without specifics. So how about meeting me for a drink in the bar downstairs tonight? Say at six o'clock? Just a short one," Girard said.

"Sure. I'll see you then." In the background, she could see Giselle waiting impatiently, wearing black high-heeled boots, a short black skirt, and a tight black-and-white-checked T-shirt, with a black leather jacket slung over her shoulders.

"Looks like Giselle is waiting for you. I'll see you later on." Luz turned around to walk the other way.

After dinner the night before, Luz had done a quick internet search of Girard Morel and Giselle Mouton. Giselle was everywhere—her photos of every major racing event worldwide were posted along with celebrities at charity events from practically every continent. A true jetsetter, Giselle practiced a form of tolerant rudeness to anyone who was not a member of the A-list. And Girard Morel, also a Frenchman, showed up as an also-ran on the list of financial brokers in America. One article termed his firm a bucket shop and said his last big project, four to five years before, had been an accidental success. There were a few articles that hinted at bankruptcy in the future for GMB Financial, unless there was a significant infusion of funds. Many commented that he had done his last big deal—not a recommendation anyone would want from his peers.

Were they in Sonoma at the track because of Sacha Bernard? He was an A-lister. Or was their presence related to the murder of Orval Slattery and the absence of Paul Angel at Chateau La Mer?

Luz had one more day before Detective Boone arrived to meddle in the circumstances related to Orval's death. She had only a few hours before she would have to turn everything over to an expert. Hopefully she'd find something that would lead her to whoever poisoned the wine that killed Orval Slattery.

CHAPTER 15

Driving to the track through the grassy, wheat-colored hills, Luz focused on what Jeff said to her the night before. All the intrigue with Chateau La Mer distracted her from the various jobs she needed to do for the team and kept her from concentrating on the tasks Jeff counted on her to do. As she flashed her parking pass and found her way to the lot where team members parked, Luz saw that Sacha Bernard's Bentley was already there, as was Clint and Michelle's convertible.

With Mark Miller having trouble describing his setup problems to the team, it was likely to be a very tense day. Both Christi and Mark were standing in the shade of the scoring stand, looking at the telemetry data from the day before. They were chattering about the S's, a series of turns that wound down the hill, midway through the track.

Jeff consulted with Clint, looking over the notebook filled with data from years before that reflected track condition, weather, tires, and adjustments made to the forerunners of the current chassis. Michelle and Sacha were lingering over coffee, laughing at some private joke, when Luz walked up to them.

"Practice will begin in five minutes," the track announcer boomed over the PA system.

Most of the cars were in their pit boxes, with drivers and owners hovering nearby. Christi and Mark flipped a coin to see who would go out first, and Christi won the toss. Since there was only an hour of practice before qualifying, Jeff wanted to focus on one car at a time, and then later, after qualifications, practice two-car pit stops and full-tank tests.

Up in the scoring stand, Luz, Sacha, and Michelle watched the data screens and made notes, as the engines fired up and the cars zipped out of the pits.

"Why have I not heard of this Christi before the Indy 500?" asked Sacha, as he studied the image of the full track showing each of the cars by number as they sped around the track, bunching up in the curves, and gaining speed on the straightaways where most of the drivers hoped to lose the others and move ahead in the pack.

"She is quite good—good enough for Formula International, I think." He stroked his mustache as he watched the track and the computer screens reflecting real-time data.

"Sacha, you know she has a contract with our team, don't you?" Michelle asked, arching her eyebrow at him as she sat up straight and pushed her shoulders back authoritatively.

"Yes, I have heard such, but I also know it is not forever," he said archly.

Michelle glared at him and raised her voice. "She has to get our permission to drive for anyone else, even if it is a test."

"Michelle, I have no intention of stealing your driver from your team, but I do think it would be worthwhile for her to try out the Formula car sometime soon," Sacha purred, "sometime very soon. You would not want to deprive her of that opportunity, would you?"

With their faces nose to nose, almost touching, and the words louder with each sentence, Luz could hear the discussion between Michelle and Sacha escalating into an argument that could be detrimental to everyone.

"Hey, look, Christi is leading the pack!" Luz said. She stood up and pointed to the Amberson-Harwood car Christi was driving, then turned to face Michelle and Sacha. "Why couldn't you consider a joint venture if she makes the grade and can move into Formula International?"

Surprise crossed their faces, and they both began to laugh as they realized how close they'd been to a fight. Sacha chuckled, "*Voilà*! A brilliant idea!" and said to Michelle, "Luz is a marvel—I understand now how you won at Indy. Her ideas are so creative. As we say in France, '*Vive la différence!*'"

With the two old friends now amiably discussing what that business partnership would be like, Luz stepped down from the scoring stand and stood next to Jeff as he waited for Christi to come into the pit box.

"Hey, what's going on up there?" Jeff asked.

"Oh, just planning your next big deal," Luz said. "Maybe moving up to Formula International. Who knows?"

"Really?"

"They're hashing out the details now. Don't think about it—let's worry about this race first." Luz peered down at the computer screen to look at the data.

Jeff looked puzzled, then nodded. Christi started up the pit road, and Mark Miller readied himself for his minutes in the car. During the driver change, Luz watched the team, timed the stop, and looked at the weather forecast for race day. When she looked up from her notes, a yellow car, number 66, caught her eye as it sped down the pit road. She followed it up to a pit box far to the front of the pit lane, and decided to do a little research after Mark went out for practice.

With her sunglasses on, her hat pulled low over her face, and her hair tucked into the crown of it, Luz walked purposefully down pit row past the other pit boxes, carefully observing her surroundings. She knew Roger Schneider was at the track and was watching the car in practice. What she didn't know would hurt her and the Amberson-Harwood team, and that was what she had to try to find out before qualifying.

Roger still held a grudge about how the Indy 500 had turned out. Although he was using laundered money to finance his team, Roger had testified against his partner, Mauricio, Luz's former boyfriend, in order to avoid charges that would forever bar him from the sport of auto racing. Luz knew Roger blamed her for being shot by Mauricio in the men's room of the garage area just as the Amberson-Harwood team finished first and second at the 500 the preceding May.

Walking by the pit stall for the yellow number 66 car, Luz confirmed her hunch: this was the Blackbird Racing team entry. All the familiar faces, including Roger Schneider's, were present. Just as she turned to go into the paddock area where the transporters were lined up, one by one, Luz heard Roger Schneider say, "Hey, Girard, thanks for coming out to the track. Glad they gave you credentials without a hassle."

Turning to see where he was, Luz found herself facing a pit cart towing a rack of tires, so she stepped out of the way, behind a tall stack of rims, and used the opportunity to watch the two men greet each other. Roger slapped Morel on the back, shaking his hand and laughing as he mentioned his big win and gain at the auction the previous night. Roger said, "Oh, I'll get more… How is the stock deal going, by the way?"

At this point some engines started—a few cars were leaving the pits—and Luz could not hear the rest of the conversation. Her intuition told her she still had to worry about the safety of the team on the track. At the same time, she was also still concerned about Sara and Chateau La Mer.

She walked through the garage area to the trailer, where she checked the fire suits the team would wear during the race, making sure all the companies paying contingency money were represented properly and in the right place on the uniforms. No point in the team losing money when it was easy to earn it if the contract stipulations for the sanctioning body and the sponsors were followed. Luz found that a few sponsors' logos were missing, so she went in search of the much-sought-after patches that she would sew on before the race.

When she returned to the scoring stand, Jeff accosted her. "Where have you been? I've been looking for you. A new sponsor I've been working on for months just decided to sign with us today." He shoved a plastic bag filled with logoed patches at Luz. "We have to get these patches on all the team shirts before qualifying, which starts in thirty minutes."

At the same time, he handed her a bunch of shirts, saying harshly, "These patches go on the left side of the front down below the one for Waxworks Car Wash. OK?" He pointed out the location on the front of the red team shirts and turned his back on her to talk to the team engineer.

Luz was stunned. Jeff had never talked to her like she was his personal servant before. She looked up at the scoring stand, only to see Michelle, Sacha, and Giselle seated on the scoring stand. Giselle waved at Luz haughtily while she asked Michelle and Sacha to pose for a selfie of the three together. Giselle pointed to something on the track, and they all turned in that direction, oblivious to the interchange between Jeff and Luz. Taking a deep breath, Luz walked back to the transporter with the patches and the shirts, hoping to find her sewing kit on the top shelf of the cupboards where she'd left it after Indy, the last race when she'd been with Jeff.

Fortunately it was still there, so she found a place at one of the tables in the shade of the transporter's canopy and settled down to sew the patches on. With only a few minutes to go, Luz quickly pinned them on, put a few stitches in strategic places, just enough to keep them on the shirts for the next hour or so, and worked her way through the ten shirts Jeff gave her. Not sure if she needed to have the logo on her shirt as well, Luz found a couple of safety pins in the kit, and quickly added the patch where it belonged. She ran out of the garage to the pit area and handed the shirts out to the mechanics, who stripped their old shirts off, to the delight of the women in the crowd, and put the newly decorated shirts on just in time for the announcement that qualifications were starting.

With qualifying order determined by practice times, fastest to slowest, Christi and Mark were in the first group to go out on the track. Unlike at Indy, each car only had one chance to qualify, so everyone was crossing their fingers that all the team's practice would pay off.

Luz mounted the scoring stand and watched the telemetry, making notes of anything Jeff pointed out to her while the drivers made their way around the track. Their warm-up laps were good, and the two laps for qualifying were faster than their best practice times. Mark was slightly faster than Christi, surprising the team. It seemed he'd finally figured out how to get through the S-turns without losing too much speed.

After the cars came in from their qualifying laps, the team towed them over to the tech line, where they were checked to make sure they were in compliance with the specifications described in the rulebook: the height of the back wing, the level of the engine cowling, and the clearance under the chassis, to name a few.

The times both drivers ran were among the fastest ever at the track, so assuming the cars made it through tech, Luz knew they were safely in the field, as long as there was not an accident during practice later in the day. The race was the next day, so Luz gathered the shirts and took them back to the transporter, planning to work on them later, after they'd been laundered. Quickly she began to place the patches on the fire suits so they would be ready in the morning when the team prepared the pits for the race.

When the team towed the cars back into the canopied area by the transporter, where they would have lunch, talk about qualifying, and get ready for one more practice that day, Luz was there finishing up her work. Bent over her phone, she looked at the qualifying order and saw that the Blackbird car would be in the row behind Christi and Mark.

Jeff walked up to the table, jostling her arm as he sat down. She frowned as she looked up to see who was causing her to lose her place on the screen.

"Don't look so grumpy. We really qualified well. Sorry, I didn't mean to sound so gruff out there, but I couldn't find you, and those patches had to be on the shirts or we would have lost the sponsorship. Forgive me?"

Luz felt like she was being whipsawed. Jeff was harsh with her one minute and sweet the next. Was it just because they'd been apart for a few months? Had he changed, or had she? Sighing deeply, Luz chose her next words carefully. "Thanks for the apology. I'm concerned because the Blackbird car is right behind ours for the start, and because Schneider is up to something involving Chateau La Mer and maybe our team. Considering what happened at Indy, I am naturally suspicious."

She took a breath. "Is this his first race back? Or have you seen him at the other races this summer?"

At first Jeff was expecting Luz to blast him with an angry retort, but her calm, clear response prompted him to think seriously about what she'd said.

"I'll make sure the garage area is secured tonight after practice, just in case Roger or his team members, have any plans to sabotage our cars."

"Same guys. Every one of them. Thank you for listening to my concerns and looking after the cars," Luz said. "I also think Christi and Mark need company wherever they go. Big company, if you know what I mean."

Jeff asked, "Are you sticking around for practice this afternoon?"

"I'd really like to meet Sara at Chateau La Mer. There is some research I need to do there, and the sooner the better, I think. I don't have much time left to figure out what is going on before Detective Boone arrives. He may already be here, for all I know."

"I figured you had something planned, when I saw you were working on the fire suits."

"Look, I really don't like to be caught flat-footed. Especially by you." Luz smiled at him. "So I figured I needed to get that done yesterday."

Jeff grimaced. "Yeah, I wasn't very nice. Sorry. I guess I don't like needing anyone to help me. Is there any chance we could have dinner tonight, or is there another party I've forgotten about?"

"Another party. This one is the Charity Calcutta, where the drivers are auctioned off and paired with the bidders. The winning driver/bidder pairing gets to donate the money raised to the charity of their choice, which will be announced after the race tomorrow."

"OK, then, how about you go with me?" Jeff asked. "What time will you be ready?"

"I'd love to be your date. Let's meet at the bar in the lobby around six-thirty tonight, and we can go from there. I'll be at Chateau La Mer until I come back to change for the party. It's casual dress, but local wineries are donating the food and drinks, so it will be another feast." Luz put away the sewing kit and gathered her backpack and sunglasses.

When Luz began walking to the parking area, Jeff fell in beside her. When she reached her car, he helped her put the pack in the trunk, opened the door for her, and put his arm around her. Leaning against the car, he kissed her. "Be careful, Luz. Lots of traffic on the roads, and besides, you are looking for a murderer. I'm counting on being with you tonight."

Closing the door after she was seated, he bent down and gave her another soft, tender kiss. When she pulled out of the parking lot, looking in her rearview mirror, she saw him waving goodbye.

CHAPTER 16

The road leading to the Chateau La Mer winery undulated through the low hills outside St. Helena. Getting to that part of the wine country required Luz to drive through the mountains from Sonoma on the Oakville Grade, with its sweeping views and cliff-edge drop-offs. As she entered the La Mer property, Luz noticed the duck pond to the left. Next to it there was a bandstand and a shady stone patio where guests were enjoying wine served to them by a youthful sommelier.

After parking her car, she walked toward the limestone structure built into the hillside. The signage there announced that she could go to the right for the self-guided winery tour, to the left to the business offices, and straight ahead for the tour group check-in and wine tasting appointments. Luz was tempted by the self-guided winery tour, but instead went looking for Sara at the business offices. Pushing the oak and glass door open, Luz found the offices furnished with old-country antiques mixed in with stylish yet comfortable chairs in car-amel-colored Italian leather. The walls were decorated with well-used metal tools and with sepia photographs showing winemaking in the area at the turn of the century. She intro-duced herself to the young man at the reception desk, explain-ing that she had arranged to meet with Sara Slattery. While she waited, Luz perused the shelves where she found books, photographs, and carefully framed tasting notes from days gone by.

A black-and-white photograph on one of the upper shelves caught her eye; it was of three swarthy young men in white shirts, bandannas tied around their necks, wineglasses in hand. Behind them, wooden casks were stacked high against a pale limestone wall. She stretched high to reach the photo, to get a closer look, when she heard an unfamiliar male voice behind her ask, "May I?"

Startled by the man's catlike presence, Luz cleared her throat. "Please," she said, and long fingers grasped the frame easily. Turning to her right, she looked into the eyes of a tall man, his bald head gleaming as if it were made of marble. She thanked him as he handed her the image.

"That's an old one. I haven't really looked at it closely be-fore, just noticed it in passing through this room," he said. "Must have been a group of pickers after the harvest. So many migrant farmworkers were needed to get the grapes in before all the mechanized equipment we have now. So inefficient." After handing her the framed photograph, he clapped the dust off his hands as if to be rid of what it represented. As he placed one of his hands in the pocket of his slacks, a keychain with the initials, PA, fell onto the floor. Quickly he scooped them up, turned to Luz and nonchalantly asked, "And why are you here? I thought you were with those track people."

"I'm here to see Sara Slattery. We're friends from San Antonio."

"I see," he said. He then spoke loudly to the receptionist, "Reynaldo, see if you can get Sara on the phone."

"I just called her, when Ms. Dane arrived, but there was no answer. I thought maybe she was with you."

While the two men discussed Sara's possible whereabouts, Luz scrutinized the photograph. There was something familiar about two of the men pictured in it, and suddenly she realized those two men were Orval Slattery and Sacha Bernard. So perhaps the third man was Paul Angel: was this a rare photograph of that famous winemaker? Luz had to find a way to make a copy of it, or somehow capture the image. She thought about it and chuckled: yes, she had a little spy camera with her; so did everyone else, nowadays. She took out her phone, captured the image several times, and sent the photos to herself and Sacha with the question "Anyone you know?"

Dressed for work in the fields, Orval had a youthful, relaxed appearance, different from the image of him in the photograph at his house that Luz had seen just a few days before. He was thinner in this image, too, reminding her of how hard the war had been on so many people.

Looking at the image on her phone, she noticed a faint stenciled coat of arms on the end of one of the wine casks, and the letters *B-E-R-N* below. Of course, Luz realized this photo was taken at Chateau Bernard in France during the war, when the Bernard family was hiding Orval among their workers and Paul Angel was both working for the Resistance and learning from Sacha's father how to make wine.

Just then she heard the tall man say her name, so she quickly exited her photos and put her phone in her pocket. She looked up at him, carefully studying his face. He didn't look like an older version of the third man in the photo.

"Yes, you found Sara?" Luz asked. She held the framed picture out for him to take it.

He glanced down at the photo, and his face paled, seeing a youthful image of a much younger man whom he did not resemble in height, bone structure, or facial features. Then he looked hard at Luz, wondering why she was so interested in seeing the photograph.

"Why did you want to see this photograph?" he asked.

"I love old photos. Often they capture scenes from everyday life that were forgotten long ago. As you said, just some migrant workers after a long day's work," she said in a casual tone.

"Sara does not seem to be answering her phone, but then again, she may be in one of the cellars, and there is no cell reception deep underground. I'll take you to her office, and she'll be along soon, I am sure," he said carefully. He glanced at the photo again.

"Don't you want to put it back, where it was originally on display?" Luz asked, wondering about his strange behavior since she'd handed him the photo.

The man looked up from the picture, staring at Luz as if she was speaking a foreign language, then realized that even Reynaldo, hovering nearby, was perplexed by his behavior. The receptionist was motioning to him that the frame belonged on the top shelf.

"Um, yes, certainly." He glided over to the shelves in the reception area and carefully returned the photo to its original spot.

"Sorry, I must have been lost in thought—there is so much going on this weekend. We have a brunch and several tastings, and so many visitors. Who would have thought people interested in auto-racing are also interested in wine?" He babbled on while Luz and Reynaldo awkwardly stood by.

Finally he said, "This way, please," and pointed down a long corridor, adding, "Third door on the right. Wonderful view of the duck pond. Sara will be right along, I'm sure."

Luz followed his directions and found herself in what must have been Orval Slattery's office. Now she had a chance to look around. In this room Luz felt the presence of the old man she'd known for years. Outfitted with a desk made from an antique door fitted with a glass top, the office also had a sitting area with a sofa and comfortable chairs. More photographs littered the walls, and Luz searched for another image of what she was now calling "Sara's Three Musketeers." She hoped to find a more recent image of the three men, one that showed Orval's snow-white hair, Sacha's salt-and-pepper mustache, and Paul Angel looking his current age.

It was close to four o'clock in the afternoon when Luz spotted another photo that might be what she had in mind. This photo, like the other, was sitting on a top shelf. Not wanting to ask anyone for help, she moved a spindly wooden chair to the credenza, hoping she could gently use it to get to the framed picture. Taking off her shoes, she stepped up on the chair and quickly grabbed for the photo. As she attempted to hop down, though, she heard a cracking sound, and the base collapsed under her weight, causing her to drop the photo. The frame broke, and the glass shattered. On her hands and knees, Luz searched for the photo, hoping all the noise hadn't aroused the occupants of the neighboring offices.

"What was that noise?" Luz heard the man who directed her to Orval's office ask. "What are you doing on the floor?" He was looking at the broken chair, at Luz with her shoes off, and up at the shelves, wondering what she had been doing.

Thinking fast, Luz said, "Um, my feet hurt from all the standing and walking I've been doing at the track, so I sat on that chair to take my shoes off, and it just collapsed under my weight. I guess I need to go on a diet. I'll pay to have the chair repaired."

She gave him a very embarrassed and sad look, hoping he would leave her alone so she could find the photo.

He came over to her, offered her his hand, and hoisted her up. "Good thing you didn't break anything else besides the chair. This office has all kinds of rare, collectible items that I can't afford to lose."

Luz thought about his possessive attitude, talking like it was his office and these were his things. It didn't jibe with someone who was an employee of Orval and Sacha's who up until recently supposedly made wine for a living.

This man was visibly perturbed, his eyes darting around the room like he suspected something was missing. In an annoyed tone, he said, "Since Sara is not back yet, either she didn't remember you had an appointment or she is not coming back today. The facilities are only open another hour, so why don't you come back another time?"

Luz sat down on the sofa and picked up one of her shoes, shaking it out in case glass had fallen inside. She looked at him, studying his face while she tried to figure out where the photo might be. As she moved her leg up to slip on one of her shoes, she heard a crack behind her, and realized she was sitting on the frame, so she stayed where she was and nodded to him, as she said,

"Yes, I think you may be right. Sara has so much going on, she may have forgotten we were going to get together, so I'll come back later this weekend. Now I'm going to put on my shoes, and write her a note about the chair, and then I'll be gone."

He hesitated, but Luz assured him that it would only take a couple more minutes, and then she would leave. He turned and left the room, giving Luz a chance to sit up, grab the frame stuck between the sofa cushion and her back, and sweep away the shards of glass from the photo so she could give it a quick look. A color photo, taken at what looked to be a party, showed the three men together around a piano—the piano in Orval's house, where Luz had seen the first photo of the three men. Orval had built the house ten years before, so maybe this was a housewarming party. Capturing this image on her phone, she emailed it to herself and to Sacha, where she would take the time later to look at the image. She knew she had to get out of the office quickly, before anyone came back to bother

her again.

Finding a small notepad and pen, Luz wrote a quick note to Sara apologizing for breaking the chair and promising to pay for the repair. Luz hid the five-by-seven photo and its frame under the sofa, gathered the shards of glass she'd been sitting on, and threw them away.

Luz had a feeling that the tall bald man was waiting outside in the hallway to see when she would leave. She thought he probably planned to go back in to see what if anything had been disturbed. Smoothing her slacks, tucking in her shirt, and dabbing on some lip gloss, Luz left Sara's office in time to see him pop into the one next door. She waved goodbye as she walked to the reception area, nodding to Reynaldo and left the headquarters building.

Luz walked back to the duck pond area, then went over to the valet parking kiosk. The young woman there asked for her ticket.

"Oh, I'm not ready to leave yet. Have you seen Sara Slattery drive through here recently?"

"She came in right after lunchtime, and I haven't seen her car leave. In fact"—the perky attendant walked over to a gate and looked through it, then returned to Luz—"her car is parked right over there under that massive oak tree." She pointed to a vintage silver Porsche 911. "Miss Slattery says that tree reminds her of her home in Texas."

Luz nodded, making a mental note of the car, since she and Sara had come from the airport together. She assumed this was the car Orval Slattery had kept in Napa.

"Good, maybe I can find her in the winery. I still have an

hour before it closes, right?"

"Yes, you can still take the self-guided tour, and of course the grounds are open until dusk. Many people come with a picnic, buy some of our wine, and enjoy the sunset at the end of the day."

"What a great idea," Luz said. "I hope I have time later in the week to do that. Thank you for the suggestion!"

Luz walked back to the entrance to the main building and followed the signs for the self-guided tour, snagging a map and brochure along the way.

The guided tour of Chateau La Mer started with a ride in a glass elevator that rose to the top of the stone and stucco building. When she got out of the elevator, Luz found herself on a deck overlooking the vineyards of the surrounding area. She could see that most of the vines were loaded with grapes ready to be picked. In some parts of the valley the harvest had started. Here she could see equipment lined up in anticipation of when the grapes would be at their peak.

From the deck area, a ramp led her to an indoor area where all the stainless steel tanks, crushers, and destemming equipment was found. This huge indoor tank farm was sparkling clean, awaiting the grapes from this year's harvest. Luz looked down from the observation walkway thirty feet over the tanks, wondering if Sara was inspecting these areas with her staff.

As she strolled down the ramps, she stopped at the various tour destinations, where she read information plaques about how the grapes are crushed, how long they are left in the tanks, and when they begin the aging process in the French oak barrels.

Luz went from a brightly lit industrial warehouse area to a dimly lit, cavelike room furnished with tapestries and California country antiques. On a balcony to her right, she could stand and take in a view overlooking what appeared to be miles and miles of wooden casks.

As she leaned over the balcony, again looking for Sara, she sensed someone behind her, thinking it was another visitor who wanted a chance to look out over the sea of wooden casks. Just as she moved to get out of the way and continue on the tour, she felt a sharp pain in her neck. Grabbing for the balcony railing, she tried to stay upright, but then everything went black and she tumbled to the floor.

CHAPTER 17

Freshly showered, with a crisp white shirt that set off his tan, Girard Morel walked into the bar in the lobby of the hotel at six o'clock sharp and looked around. With a night of wine tasting ahead, he ordered sparkling water with lime and sipped it slowly, savoring the citrus flavor.

About fifteen minutes later, Jeff came into the bar and saw Girard, recognizing him as the man who'd flirted with Luz at the party the night before. He walked toward him and the two shook hands as if they were old friends. Jeff wore a cream linen jacket over a blue cotton dress shirt.

"Mind if I join you?" Jeff said, motioning toward the empty barstool next to Girard.

"Sure, fine. I'm waiting for someone, who appears to be late," Girard said, a bit annoyed, looking at his watch. "I thought she would have texted me to let me know if she was going to be this late."

"Well, you know women," Jeff said. "It always takes extra time to get ready for anything, even to go out to exercise. I really don't get it."

"But she's a professional," Girard said. "I would have thought she'd be here on time."

"Did she know it was a business meeting? Or did she think it was just a drink to talk, get to know each other?" Jeff asked carefully, sipping his beer.

"I thought I was clear that I was going to talk with her about a stock transaction, but there is no telling, women are so hard to read."

"Do you mean Luz Dane? Were you supposed to meet her here for a drink?" Jeff did his best to hide his burgeoning jealousy.

"Yes, the woman you were with at last night's dinner," Girard said. "I literally ran into her in the hall upstairs, and we talked for a minute and exchanged contact info. We agreed to meet here at six tonight."

"And she was going to meet me here at six-thirty, and she isn't here yet. Hmmm." Jeff took a swig of his beer, searching the room for any other familiar faces.

Jeff looked at his phone, but didn't see any texts. He turned it off and then back on again, since he was in a different location than earlier in the day and thought maybe the network didn't know where he was. Girard watched him, checked his texts, found nothing from Luz, and then rebooted his phone too.

Jeff laughed. "I wouldn't think you'd have any problems with connectivity—I mean, you have so many contacts in Sil-

VIRGIN AT SONOMA

icon Valley."

"You'd be surprised. As much as I travel, I experience the same things that everyone else does with this hardware," Girard responded, a puzzled look on his face. "Would you text her, just in case she doesn't recognize my number and so she's not responding to me?"

"I've already texted her, and no response here either." Jeff showed Morel his screen and began scanning the room again. His eyes lit up for a moment, then he waved to someone across the room.

Sara Slattery saw Jeff and Girard and walked toward them. She smiled as she recalled his bidding on the Formula International trip, which had helped break all historical charity records from previous years.

"Good to see you again, Girard," she said. "Sorry you didn't win that trip."

"Oh, but I did. Roger Schneider sold it to me for a premium. He knew I wanted it badly."

Jeff shuddered on hearing Schneider's name. Slipping off his barstool, he offered it to Sara, who gladly settled in next to Girard and ordered a glass of L'Étoile du Mer sparkling wine.

Jeff asked Sara, "Have you seen Luz? She was supposed to meet me and Girard here in the bar tonight before the party." Worry etched Jeff's face as he looked around the room, hoping he'd see Luz walk through the door.

Casually Sara answered, "She told me she was going to meet me at Chateau La Mer, but she never showed."

Sara sipped her wine, then looking at both men. "Don't worry, you two, she'll show up. Everything with her is so cloak

143

and dagger. She's probably tied up somewhere working on a stock portfolio. I know she won't miss the driver Calcutta and dinner. You worry too much, Jeff."

Sara flirtatiously tossed her long hair over her shoulder and leaned in toward Girard, leaving Jeff standing nearby with an empty beer, no date, and a puzzled expression on his face.

Jeff considered what Sara had said. It was true that this wasn't the first time Luz stood him up when she was working on something for a client. For all he knew, she had also made a date for a drink with Sacha Bernard. Ever since she had set up her own investment advisory service, Luz hadn't been quite the same. From Jeff's point of view she seemed more flighty, less focused, and more self-centered. He kept looking at his phone, hoping to see a text from her. When nothing came up on the screen, he gave up.

Jeff put his empty bottle down on the bar and patted Girard and Sara on the shoulder. "I'm going over to the party. I need to work the crowd so that Christi and Mark will go for the highest bids tonight. I'll see you two at the dinner."

CHAPTER 18

The pain at the base of her neck was excruciating. Luz tried to move her head, but the white flashes of pain were so brutal she almost blacked out again when she moved it from side to side. Her hands, bound behind her, rubbed up against a cold dirt floor. She thought she heard a faint voice say, "Careful, just rest."

Luz tried to open her eyes a slit, to see if someone was there, but she couldn't see anything. Again she heard the voice; she assumed she was imagining it.

Luz mused that if she was going to imagine a voice telling her something, it might as well be a friendly voice, telling her positive things. She asked herself, "What would my grandfather tell me to do if he found me like this?"

Tears seeped from her eyes as Luz thought of her parents, whom she'd lost so many years ago. Then she took a deep breath and started to calmly breathe in and out, as if she were meditating. She knew crying wasn't going to get her out of the pain that hurt so badly. But all she wanted to do was cry—to achieve a primitive and temporary release from the pain in her neck and her head. As she continued to breathe, Luz tried to think methodically and rationally so she could figure out where she was, why she was here, and what she could do to get away.

Searching her memory for the last experience she could recall, Luz remembered the self-guided tour of Chateau La Mer. Was she still in the winery, she wondered, or was she somewhere else?

"That's good. Steady your breathing," she heard the male voice say.

This voice had the same rhythm as that of her fraternal grandfather, whom she knew when she was a toddler. She had called him "Grampa." The comfort she derived from the voice made her wonder if she was drugged and hallucinating.

Luz focused on her breathing and did a slow, careful body check, wiggling her toes and her fingers. It felt good to stretch. Then, after first tightening and then relaxing her muscles from her feet to her shoulders, she released a few kinks in her back. When she got to her neck, the pain was too much for her, and she blacked out again.

At some point in the night she felt a blanket being spread over her. A voice said, "Sleep. Just sleep."

The next morning, cold from the floor permeated the air in the room, while sunlight filtered in from a window warming Luz where she lay. Turning her head toward the comforting but sparse heat, Luz tried to open her eyes, only to feel a blinding pain when she did so.

"Turn your head the other way, slowly now." It was that old voice again—a little hoarse, yet soothing in its softness.

"Okaaay, Grampa," Luz responded, her mouth dry and her words slurring as she uttered them. She worked to open her eyes again: it felt like they were filled with sand. Luz blinked several times, now facing away from the bright sunlight.

"I'm moving over to where you can see me, just so you'll know I'm not your Grampa," said the voice she heard inside her head.

As Luz stared at the stucco and stonewall, a wizened face appeared, atop a thin body clothed in jeans and a plaid fleece work shirt. She had seen the face before, in a photograph, she thought, but she couldn't remember for sure, nor did she know his name. Rotating her head, stopping before the sunlight attacked her eyes, Luz asked, "Where am I and who are you?"

A smile crinkled the skin around his gray eyes. "Mademoiselle, I am Paul Angel, winemaker of Chateau La Mer, at your service. And we are in a cell deep beneath the caves here at the winery."

"You didn't go away. You're alive," Luz whispered in wonder. "What are you doing here? What about that other man? And how do I know you are who you say you are?"

"I will answer all your questions and prove to you that I am, as you say, who I say I am, in a moment. Let's get you sitting up first."

Luz stared at her fellow prisoner, blinked, and slowly nodded. The pain was still there, but it had decreased a little. She thought he looked like an elf, since he was small, like a jockey, and had a kind face.

Reaching around her shoulders and pushing her up to a sitting position, he said, "We have some time to talk before breakfast is served."

As he pushed, Luz willed herself to sit up, groaning as she became upright. Wobbling a little, she straightened her back and neck, pushing her shoulders back to stretch her tight muscles.

"*Ooof*. Everything hurts," she said.

"Can you stay up by yourself while I get something to cut those plastic zip ties off your wrists?"

"Yes," Luz croaked.

Turning her head slowly, her eyes following him, Luz watched as Paul Angel, graceful as a cat, darted over to an iron bed under the window, removed the finial on the right corner of the headboard, reached into the hollow iron corner post, and retrieved what looked like a knife, then did the same on the other side. He then replaced both the finials and, stretching up to the windowsill, grabbed something small Luz could not see.

Putting all the pieces together, Paul Angel came toward her with a pair of pruning shears, kneeled down behind her, and snipped the plastic handcuffs in two, releasing Luz from her bondage.

"Oh! That feels so good." She rubbed her hands in front of her and stretched her unfettered fingers and wrists.

"Let me help you up off the floor," Paul said in a low voice, reaching down to give her a hand. "Careful, you may feel lightheaded, so first scoot over here and sit down on the bed."

Luz was unsteady on her feet, grateful there was a place to sit before she had to make it completely upright. While she steadied her breathing and stretched her sore muscles, Paul reached over to a small table and grabbed a metal thermos and a cup.

"Water?" He handed Luz the little cup. "Drink it slowly, even though you are very thirsty. It will quench your thirst better that way."

Luz took a small sip, swishing the water around in her mouth before swallowing. She took a few more sips, then handed the half-full container back to Paul.

He passed Luz a plate that held a few grapes, a bit of cheese, and a few dry crackers. "I wasn't expecting another guest. Fortunately you dropped in before I finished my evening meal, so I saved this little bit for you."

"Thank you," Luz said. "I'm really hungry. I've had nothing to eat since lunch, when? Yesterday? I don't even know what day it is or how long I've been here."

"You dropped in on me yesterday evening. As for the day of the week, I only know what day it is by when they let me out of here to go to the fields to look at the grapes. According to my records here," he said, looking at ten scratches on the wall, "I've been in this prison for ten days."

"How did you get here and why, if you get to go out each day, do you come back in here?" Luz winced as she bit into one of the dry crackers, then rubbed her neck.

"We only have until the sunlight hits that corner of the room for me to explain. That is when someone will come to bring me food and you need to get back down on the floor and pretend you are still hurt and unconscious."

"I don't understand," Luz said.

"There is a man who worked for Chateau La Mer for many years. I've known him since I was a boy in France," Paul said. "He holds it against me that his entire family died one night in France long ago. He plans to kill all of us who knew him then: Orval, Sacha, and me."

"Paul, Orval is dead. He was murdered at the Children's Home wine dinner, when he made the toast to Sara. The wine was poisoned."

Paul bent his head, as if in prayer. After a moment, he crossed himself. Then, staring into space at one corner of the room, he said, "Ah, so that is how he is going to play the game."

"What do you mean?"

"I know the man who is the murderer. He plans to kill each one of us in a way that he feels is most just for each man. He used a technique in making champagne, where a little dose of sugar, in liquid form, is added to wine to speed up fermentation and add bubbles to the wine. In Orval's case he used it to add poison to the wine instead. So easy to do through a small hole in the cork."

"I still don't understand," Luz said.

"It was my technique. I used it to kill many Germans and his family, traitors every one, when they moved into our village. His plan is for me to be blamed, tried for murder, and then executed," Paul said.

"Why now?" Luz asked.

"Because someone wants to buy the vineyards and the winery here and in France. It will make him rich, and the three of us will not live to enjoy the work of our lifetimes." Paul shook his head, and his tone grew sad. "Sacha is the one I worry about the most. His love of fast cars and beautiful women will blind him. He will not see far enough ahead to escape death once it is planned for him."

"You told me you would prove that you are really Paul Angel," Luz said, thinking back on her lunch with Sacha, when he showed her the half-angel tattoo at the base of his thumb and explained that the corresponding tattoo on Paul's hand would complete the angel image.

Paul Angel clenched his fist, holding it up for Luz to see. The outline of a halo, half a head, and one wing stood out for her to see. With his hand relaxed, it looked like a scar from long ago.

"Ah, so you *are* his trusted friend. He will be so glad you are alive."

A jingling of keys was heard coming down the hallway, so Luz quickly rolled onto the floor, resuming a prone position, with the blanket over her body, her hands behind her back. Paul Angel hid the pruning shears under the mattress and lay down as if he was dozing.

When the door opened, a woman carrying a tray of food said, "*Bonjour*, Paul. How is our guest today?"

"She is still sleeping. Did you bring enough food for both of us?"

"Yes, some fruit, bread, cheese, café au lait. Enough for two. Frederick does not want you out in the vines today. He will be in later to see you and your guest." She put the tray down and returned to the door. "*Au revoir.*"

As the door closed, Luz sat up to look at Paul. "Who was that?"

"Maurine Henrí Le Beaux. She started working here years ago, under the name of Maurine Henry. Both she and Frederick, her husband, have worked in the cellars for years."

"Maurine Henrí. Maurine Henry. She was the other witness to the codicil of Orval's will. She's his wife," Luz said, thinking out loud, trying to figure out how everything fit together. "When do you think he will be back?"

"Several hours. We must be prepared for him. Meanwhile we should eat our breakfast and sleep to keep up our strength."

While they waited, the morning sun warmed up the room and brightened their spirits. Both of them savored the café au lait and ate their breakfast while they made light conversation. Afterward, Luz curled up on the floor again, so she would be ready for Le Beaux when he returned, and Paul stretched out on the cot.

CHAPTER 19

As they were dozing in the warm sun, they heard voices, two of which were very familiar to both of them. Luz looked around the room and saw an air vent opposite the window. She motioned to Paul Angel, pointing to the air vent, cocked her head like she heard something, and then whispered, "Voices. Am I hearing voices?" she said, worried, as she touched her head tenderly. "Is that Sacha Bernard's voice?"

Paul listened carefully and nodded.

"This storeroom is next door to the caves and adjacent to the meeting room where tastings are held for private groups. There must be some kind of meeting going on," he said quietly.

Both of them sat still, listening.

Sacha Bernard's deep, rumbling voice said, "I have been asked many times about selling my shares of Chateau La Mer. From one investment banker to another, and now you, who are letting everyone think you are Paul Angel, are running *MY* winery. You, Fred Bowman, say that my friend and partner Paul has gone away. This I do not believe!"

"It is not your winery any more. I have the power to vote all shares of Chateau La Mer belonging to Paul Angel and all the shares in trust for Sara Slattery," Fred Bowman said.

Hearing the rustling of papers, and then Sacha's voice rumbling, "This is impossible. You are not Paul. Paul would not sign over his shares to anyone but one of his partners. Nor would he give anyone power over Sara's shares in trust. These documents are forged!"

Luz looked at the man she was imprisoned with and whispered, "Who is talking to Sacha ?"

"It is Frederick Le Beaux. His American name is Fred Bowman. I will tell you more later, *shh.*" Paul put his finger to his lips to silence their conversation.

An insistent voice that Luz now recognized as Fred Bowman's stated, "I will force you and Sara to sell your shares. There is no future for small wineries like Chateau La Mer or Chateau Bernard. In the past, yes, but with global competition, it is only a matter of time before this winery will go bankrupt because it cannot compete in the global market in the future!"

Luz let out an involuntary gasp, then looked at Paul Angel, who raised a finger to his lips to signal silence. They both cocked their heads toward the air vent, as if they were listening to a radio broadcast.

Then Sacha's voice bellowed, "We have competed effectively in the global markets for years. And this attachment to the will—it is a phony. The same day it was dated and signed by who knows who, Orval Slattery announced to an audience of over five hundred people that Sara would inherit his shares upon his death. This announcement was made immediately before he was murdered."

They could hear pounding on the table, then an uproar: "You are trying to steal our company. Where is Paul? Where is he hidden? Show him to me now or I will call the police!"

"You will not call the police. A scandal about your wine-maker and how he murdered his partner by poisoning him will ruin Chateau La Mer!" yelled the man calling himself Fred Bowman, "Paul is safely hidden away. I will release him after you and Sara sign your shares over to me. Then he will stand trial for the death of Orval Slattery and be sentenced to death. Just as others were sentenced to death by him."

Sacha knew that Paul Angel had enemies from his work for the Resistance. Wracking his brain for names he could remember, it dawned on him that Fred Bowman was an angli-cized version of Frederick LeBeaux. The LeBeaux family had settled in the village close to Chateau Bernard, Belgians who turned out to be Germans. Forgers by profession. How long had Fred Bowman been working at Chateau La Mer hatching his plan for vengeance against the three partners?

Paul Angel had a small half-angel tattoo on his right fist that matched the one on Sacha's left fist, joining them togeth-er as blood brothers when they were small boys, vowing never to be separated from each other. When his family was killed during the German occupation of France, Paul escaped the carnage and found his way to Chateau Bernard. There he was cared for and educated. He learned viticulture and winemaking from Sacha's father. When the wounded Orval hid among the vines to escape the Nazis, Paul and Sacha found him and hid him in plain sight as a worker in the fields. Orval, Paul, and Sacha worked together in the vineyards, preserving the ancient grapes and making wine for a world they hoped would survive to enjoy the fruits of their labors. The Bernard family did all they could to aid the French underground as they preserved the vineyards and winery.

The old man imprisoned with Luz made a fist and once again showed her the faded tattoo on his hand.

At that moment, Luz heard a soft feminine voice speak up. "I move that we call for a vote," Sara said.

"I second the motion," Sacha spoke up forcefully, "All in favor of the initial public offering of stock in Chateau La Mer Incorporated, vote by saying aye."

Luz heard the voice of Fred Bowman saying "aye." Then she heard Sacha say, "All opposed to the IPO, vote by saying *non*."

The harmony of Sara and Sacha's voices saying "*non*" in unison was beautiful, and Luz saw that Paul Angel looked relieved.

"There will be no IPO," Sacha said. "And we will not be selling you our shares! Sara, come with me. We are leaving."

At the sound of footsteps walking out the door, Luz cried out, "Help!"

Paul joined her. "Help us!"

Both of them continued to scream and yell: "Help! Help us! We are locked in the cellar!"

When they were hoarse from yelling and their hands hurt from banging on the door, Luz, feeling hopeless, curled up on the floor, sobbing. Paul sat on the cot, his head in his hands, waiting for another chance to be freed.

CHAPTER 20

Both of them dozed fitfully. Paul woke at every slight sound. For a moment he thought there was a fly in the room, which was now cooling down from the afternoon heat. He couldn't see a fly, though, and looked around, puzzled, as the buzzing sound continued.

Luz heard it too, and pulled the tail of her shirt up, producing a pouch from which she removed her cell phone. The screen was cracked, from her fall to the floor, but when she entered her security code, a torrent of text messages appeared on the screen.

In low and urgent tone, Paul said, "*Mon Dieu!* Text…text everyone you can think of. Let them know we are in the cellar. He will be here soon. You must get back on the floor, like you are hurt, and then we will work together to get away."

Luz quickly typed out a text: "HELP. In cellar at Chateau La Mer. The Angel is alive and with me. HELP." She sent it to Jeff,

Clint, Michelle, Sara, and Sacha Bernard. The battery on her phone was so low that she was afraid the message might not have been sent, but still she turned it off, hoping they could save whatever battery life there was to use later if they needed it.

Paul Angel and Luz locked eyes as they heard footsteps approaching in the stone hallway of the cellar.

Paul pointed to the floor, and Luz immediately dropped down, trying to assume the position she'd been in before she awoke. Paul covered her with the blanket he'd given her earlier, then hid his pruning shears and sat on the cot. Both of them were alert and ready to make their escape. Luz took a deep breath to relax and focus her mind on the little she had to do to help Paul. She closed her eyes, kept her hands behind her, slowed her breathing, and relaxed her body to give the impression she was still unconscious.

Soon keys rattled in the lock, the door opened, and Fred Bowman walked into the room carrying a tray with two bowls of steaming soup and some crusty bread and cheese.

"I see she is still unconscious. Maybe the smell of food will awaken her," he said.

Luz worked to keep her face slack as if she was still unconscious. Paul nodded. "Yes, at least she's still alive. I worried that you hit her too hard and she was slowly dying."

Still holding the tray, Bowman moved closer to Luz, "Let me take a look at her. Maybe she just needs help waking up?"

As he leaned over to place the tray on a small table next to where Luz was laying on the floor, he turned his back to Paul Angel. While Bowman was cantilevered forward, Paul yelled,

"NOW!" and Luz kicked the tray upward, showering Bowman with the hot soup.

"*Agh!,*" he screamed, frantically trying to wipe the scalding liquid off his face.

While his eyes were closed, Luz kicked him in the shin and knees, sending him sprawling backward, where Paul Angel hit him in the jaw, his fist wrapped around the shears, knocking him out cold.

Paul reached down to pull Luz up from the floor, then grabbed a small leather binder from under the mattress of the bed in the cell and followed Luz as she ran out the door. Seeing the keys still in the lock, Paul closed the door and locked it, taking the keys with him. Confident they wouldn't run into any resistance, he followed Luz down the hall, where she stopped in front of three doorways, not sure which way to go. Paul pointed to the last door on the left, which opened to a stairway. Paul showed Luz the keys in his hand. "Locking him up should give us a clear way out, but I don't know who else is in on this plan to take over the winery. Let's keep going."

"OK," Luz said, her voice ragged, "but can we slow down a little? My head is starting to hurt, and I'm feeling a little weak."

"A bit, but I want to get out of the building as fast as we can. Only three more flights of stairs before we get to the loading dock and out into the vineyard."

At the bottom of the stairs, Paul stopped Luz before the door that would take them into the cavernous warehouse space where all the grapes came in to be processed. It was a forest of stainless steel vats. Hoses snaked between them, creating an obstacle course Luz and Paul would have to cross to reach the exit.

"I hope we will find the room empty," Paul said. "If we're lucky, the staff is working among the vines to prepare for the harvest. But if we encounter resistance, remember to run out the door and toward the wooded area on your left."

Luz nodded her head, catching her breath as Paul opened the door. After looking around, he motioned for her to follow. Once she was alongside him, Paul grabbed her hand and guided her through the six-inch hoses winding along the slippery tile floor so they could hide behind one of the twenty-feet-tall stainless steel vats. When he was sure there was no one in the room, he walked her through the large open warehouse doors, and they sneaked between the large trucks parked in the loading area. As soon as they were out in the open, he pointed toward the wooded area and the small creek.

"We don't have time to stop right now. We have to get to your car. What does it look like and where did you park it?" Paul said.

"Red BMW convertible. Around near the front by the duck pond." Luz gasped, almost out of breath, as she tried to keep up with Paul. "Isn't there somewhere we can just lean against a tree or something?"

Paul looked behind him, and his face paled. "It's Bowman with Maurine Henry. He's just come out of the loading dock. He must have called for help on his cell phone. Hurry, let's go!"

CHAPTER 21

Without Luz at the Calcutta and the dinner afterward, Jeff became increasingly irritable and worried. Everyone who saw him—Sacha, Clint, Michelle, Girard, Sara—all asked him where she was. Not only was she ignoring his texts, she wasn't returning his phone calls either. With all the tech billionaires at the track, she probably got swept off her feet with promises of big accounts and a luxurious lifestyle.

She still hadn't arrived at the charity event by ten o'clock, so Jeff went back to the hotel where everyone was staying, thinking maybe he'd see her in the bar or getting out of a Ferrari as arm candy for some other guy.

Before he parked his car, he drove around the parking lot, looking for the red BMW convertible he remembered seeing her drive at the track. Problem was, with this group of fans, there were quite a few red cars and quite a few convertibles. He just had to let go of worrying about Luz. The race was the next afternoon, and he needed to focus on the cars, on his drivers, and get ready to at least make a decent showing, if not win the race.

Roger Schneider made another big impression that night, trying to outbid everyone for the top drivers in the Calcutta auction, which again broke fund-raising records. The people who invested in the drivers who finished on the podium at the end of the race would share the privilege of dividing up the pool of money raised between the charities of their choice and those of the drivers'. Over a million dollars changed hands that night, and six of the wine country's charities were going to get the benefit of that haul.

Where did Schneider get all his money? Jeff was puzzled, as always, at how easy it was for Roger to con people into putting money into his team. Then there was the issue of how well his cars would do against Jeff's and whether there would be any foul play involved. It was the same team that Roger had had at Indy, and the same equipment. Or, at least, that is what Jeff thought.

And why was Girard Morel cuddling up to Schneider? Couldn't he see what a scumbag he was? How did he figure into whatever Roger was scheming?

Jeff scanned the bar and the lobby before he went up to his room. He didn't see her anywhere. He thought about going to her room and banging on the door to see if she was there, but he thought better of it. Maybe she was locked in her room with a new lover, ordering room service and trying every sex position imaginable. He really didn't want to interrupt if that was the case.

Not knowing where Luz was or what she was doing was breaking his heart. He couldn't handle the idea of her running off with someone else while he waited around for her.

He checked his phone one last time for texts and calls from Luz. Nothing. He looked at his screen saver, a picture of the two of them together at Indy. Then, angry and frustrated, he turned his phone off.

CHAPTER 22

Driving to the Sonoma Raceway as dawn broke over the mountains, Jeff focused on the day ahead. Hopefully one more shakedown practice would prove the cars were ready to go and would not result in any problems—a leak, a spinout, a full-blown accident. The crew planned to meet him at the track to set up the pit areas with all the equipment that was legally permitted: fuel tank, scoring stand, extra sets of tires, gas canister for the airjack, fully loaded toolboxes, and a few chassis parts.

He hoped he would find Luz waiting for him at the track. The day before, she'd sewn all the patches on the fire suits and the team shirts. They had gone over the contingency money and gathered the stickers, placing them on the cars right before qualifying, and no new sponsors were being added for the race, so that task was handled.

More than anything, though, he wanted her there. Her

presence calmed him. He knew if she were with him, whatever crisis arose would be addressed as professionally and as imaginatively as possible. Driving into the garage area, he looked around at the parking lot, hoping to see her car. He sighed, still angry with her about being a no-show last night, but now wondering what she was up to, why she wasn't at the track working side by side with him, smiling happily and looking out for the team in her very own protective wolverine fashion.

He'd stopped at a local bakery for a box of sweet pastries—neither the donuts the guys usually enjoyed on race morning nor the breakfast tacos from Indy, but something special to go along with the gourmet coffees he'd ordered for each team member. Setting the pits up would be a more pleasant chore for everyone with these treats available only in Sonoma.

Surprisingly, when Jeff arrived he saw Sacha Bernard seated at a café table he'd set up under the awning of the transporter, reading the paper, sipping coffee, and smoking a cigarette. He was dressed in the livery of his Formula International Racing team. Sara Slattery, also drinking coffee, looked at the business section of the paper and smiled broadly as she greeted him.

"Good morning, Jeff! Isn't it a glorious day?"

"*Oui, c'est magnifique!*" Sacha added, waving casually at Jeff and then returning to his newspaper.

Jeff said, "You're both here so early. What's up?"

"Oh, we had a meeting at Chateau La Mer," Sacha answered.

"A very good meeting," Sara said, smiling.

"Yes, we made a very important business decision, and we believe this day will get even better for everyone." Sacha grinned.

Jeff made a mental note to be more open to what he could learn from this savvy Frenchman, who obviously observed the "early to rise" principle. Perhaps that had made him healthy, wealthy, and wise.

Inside the transporter, Jeff found most of the crew in their team uniforms, looking over the notes made during practice and qualifying. Christi and Mark were chatting quietly in a corner, talking about the carousel turns that often resulted in a slowdown on the track, or an accident with cars going downhill off track. Mark was still having trouble with some of the road-racing nuances that Christi had instinctively mastered.

"OK, you two, I hope the Calcutta bidding isn't a curse for today's race. You guys landed at the top, and soon we'll find out which charities you'll pick," Jeff said.

"I'm not thinking about that right now—like you said, don't want to jinx it. We're just talking over the track," Christi said, then turned back to Mark.

Jeff placed the box of pastries and the coffees on a worktable inside the transporter where the team could find them once they were finished setting up the pit stall. Most of the equipment was out and set up already. Looking around, Jeff asked the mechanics coming back from the pits, "Have you seen Luz? I thought I'd run into her here."

"The guard told me I was the first one here at the track today," answered Bart, the team's jack-man.

Jeff decided to clear his mind of Luz and work through

his list, checking off the tasks he needed to do before practice started in thirty minutes. The cars were towed out to the pit road, and while Jeff leaned down to look at the headers, he heard Clint and Michelle chatting as they approached the scoring stand. Sacha Bernard joined them shortly. A moment later Michelle looked at her cell phone. "Oh, my God!"

Clint asked, "What is it, Michelle? What's wrong?" Then his own phone sounded off with a revving-engine ring tone.

"It's Luz. Look at your phone—she's been kidnapped!" Michelle said. "How can we help her?"

Sacha's cell vibrated in the pocket of his jacket, so he too took a look. "*Mon Dieu! C'est un miracle*! Paul Angel is alive! He and Luz are trapped against their will at Chateau La Mer!"

"We have to do something!" Michelle said. She ran over to Jeff and tugged on his shirtsleeve. "We've got to get to Luz. She may be hurt! And Paul Angel too—they both are held in bondage!"

Jeff shrugged and shook his head. "Michelle, I am really mad at her. She stood me up last night, didn't show at the Calcutta party. She didn't call, she didn't text, and now you tell me she is with some other guy and they are into bondage. I'm not going to worry about her right now—I've got to get ready for this race."

Michelle looked at him like he was crazy, then looked back at her phone. "Jeff, have you checked your phone this morning? Luz is in serious trouble." Michelle knew that even an exceptional man like Jeff could be childish and jealous for no reason, just like Clint, so for now she would give him the benefit of the doubt.

"You bet she's in serious trouble, with me! My phone hasn't pinged or vibrated or anything since last night," Jeff said. Then it dawned on him. "Oh—since last night, when I completely turned it off."

"*Duh!*" Michelle said, rolling her eyes. "Right! And she's not 'into bondage'—she and Paul have been kidnapped. You fool!" Then she looked up Chateau La Mer on the map on her phone.

Jeff turned his phone on, and as soon as it secured a network connection, he got the two texts from Luz, along with a few others that team members had sent just minutes before.

"Oh, my God! Trapped in a wine cellar? Paul Angel, who's he? How far away is it?" Jeff said.

"About thirty to forty-five minutes from here," Michelle said.

Clint looked at Michelle. "Then I guess we better go get her so we can be back in time for the race."

"I will go get Paul and Luz," Sacha announced.

Jeff looked directly at Sacha. "What? Who do you think you are? Trying to steal my girlfriend, just like you tried to steal Michelle away from Clint?"

Sacha looked at Michelle, who had a seductive smile on her face, then at Clint, who was attempting not to laugh, and then at Jeff, who was red in the face and pumped up with anger. "Jeff, as much as I admire your lovely Luz, and she is one of the most intelligent women I have met, and as much as I adore the sensual Michelle too, I am not trying to 'steal' your girlfriend. My interests lie elsewhere at this moment. So please do me the honor of permitting me to find and rescue

Luz and my dear friend Paul Angel before someone tries to kill them both."

Jeff sheepishly answered, "Yes, of course. I'm sorry." He drew a deep breath and tried to calm himself. "Kill them? What do you mean?"

"Isn't it obvious to you that imprisonment in a cellar at a winery is a bit extreme?" Sacha asked, "I think I know who is behind this, but first I have to get to Luz and Paul and make sure they are safe. My Bentley is very fast, I know the area near the winery well, and no one will question my presence at Chateau La Mer."

Sacha said to Jeff, "You must stay here to make sure Christi does well in practice and makes a good showing in the race. I believe she is the future of the Formula International Racing series."

Jeff's eyebrows rose, and he started to say something, but Clint put his hand on Jeff's forearm, as if to say, "Not now."

Sacha then told Clint and Michelle, "You stay here. That way, if I cannot find Paul and Luz, you can coordinate our next steps."

"Sacha's right," said Sara, getting up from her chair and joining the group. "He's the one who should go after them. He's got connections here in the valley if there are any problems that need to be sorted out."

With that, Sacha Bernard ran across the garage area, jumped in his Bentley convertible, and, spraying gravel, shot off to Chateau La Mer to rescue Luz and his longtime partner.

CHAPTER 23

Earlier Paul had given Luz careful directions out of the cellar, so that if he could not get away to guide her, she could still find the stairway that would take her out to the back of the winery, near the loading dock. From there he instructed her to follow the small creek that flowed east to west on the property, reminding her to move away from the sun, allowing her to get back to the small lot where her car was parked. They agreed to meet along that driveway if they were separated for any reason. Luz, fearing the wooziness from her head injury would return once she was up and moving, made Paul promise that if she could not keep up, he would go without her.

Luz ran as fast as she could, following the little creek, hoping they weren't visible from the winery. She could see the driveway up ahead, behind a wild area filled with flowers and blooming shrubs.

Moving toward the duck pond, Luz saw the little red convertible glistening in the sunshine. Just about one hundred yards more, and they would be able to escape. Luz punched the button to unlock the car when they were twenty-five feet away.

"Do you feel up to driving, Luz?" Paul asked.

"Yes, once I'm in the car, I'll be OK. If you could direct me out of here, and hand me one of those bottles of water from the backseat and a protein bar from the glove box, we'll be good to go." Luz opened the car door, slid into the driver's seat, and handed Paul her phone. "You are my copilot, navigator, and in charge of communications."

Quickly she backed out of the parking place, made a reverse 180-degree turn, and pointed the car toward the roadway running between Oakville and Napa. Out of the corner of her eye, she could see Bowman running back toward the loading dock, and heard him shout, "Get me a car, a truck, anything! I've got to go after them!"

Luz stomped on the gas, working the sports car's gears to get it to maximum speed, and, at the roadway, made a left turn toward Napa.

At the first right she floored it, leaving rubber on the pavement and smoke in the air. She drove into the mountains, toward Sonoma and the track. She was on the Oakville Grade, taking each hairpin turn at the fastest speed she could handle, whipping the car through the curves.

Holding the phone this way and that, Paul searched for a cell signal but found none.

"I was afraid of that. The phone worked for that one moment while we were in the building because of the Wi-Fi, but now we are in a dead zone and the cell networks are weak at best. As we move through the mountains any chance of a signal will be blocked. I'll have to wait until we get to the other side to call for help," he said.

"The water is in the back seat, and if you could unwrap one of those bars from the glove box I'd appreciate it," Luz said, checking her rearview mirror, glad she did not see anyone following them.

Paul uncapped the water bottles and gave Luz one of the two energy bars. He quickly ate his, gulping water as a chaser. Then he focused on the battery level of the phone and willed the stairstep of bars to increase so they could call for help.

Luz concentrated on her driving, careful not to drive too close to the edge of the road. Recent rains had washed out a few of the corners, slowing down their progress.

Just as they made it to the top of the mountain and began their descent to the west side of the hillside, Paul looked in his passenger side mirror and saw a black Mercedes about fifty yards behind them and gaining speed.

"Luz, look out behind you. Bowman is gaining on us. He'll probably try to run us off the mountain. There is no place to pass up here."

Remembering some of the comments Christi and Mark had made about winning a road race, and making it through the carousel of S-curves without being forced off the road, Luz focused on looking ahead as she drove the curvy tarmac down the mountain, watching for an exit plan.

Noticing that the cell reception had improved, Paul started to make calls to the recent numbers on Luz's phone. First he dialed Jeff, where the call went immediately to voicemail. Leaving a message seemed a waste of time, but Paul did so anyway.

"Hello, Jeff. Luz and I are on our way to the track. We're being chased by Fred Bowman. We think he murdered Orval Slattery. We'll be leaving the Oakville Grade in a few minutes and then merging onto state highway 12, then to state highway 121. Please call the Sonoma County sheriff and have him send help!"

Then he called Michelle, who answered immediately. Paul gave her the same information, and she promised she would call the sheriff as soon as she got off the phone with him. She also mentioned Sacha was coming to rescue them, so she would call him and let him know where they were.

While Paul tried to dial the phone as the car swung back and forth, slaloming down the mountain, Luz mostly kept her eyes on the road in front of her but occasionally glanced in her rearview mirror. Bowman was gaining on her at every turn, probably because he knew the area, but she was not going to give up. Looking at the second hand on the dashboard clock, Luz noticed the interval in seconds between her and Bowman.

As they made their way down the Oakville Grade, getting closer to Sonoma, Luz noticed there were more homes and driveways on the downhill side of the mountain. If Bowman tried to run her off the road or pass her and block her way, she'd need to be ready to make a move that would save their lives.

Making one last call, this one to Sacha, Paul exclaimed, "*Mon ami*! We are free. Racing down the Oakville Grade with that maniac following us. Michelle is calling the sheriff. We hope to make it to Sonoma alive."

"*Sacrebleu*! He has already killed Orval. He will try to kill you. Luz is driving, yes? I have faith in her. God did not bring you this far to have you die now. I will pray for you both, my dear friend," Sacha said, his voice breaking off as the phone's battery died.

At that moment, Luz was several short turns in front of Bowman, and neither could see the other's car, so she swung the car abruptly to the left, into a driveway she'd decided would work as their escape route. She downshifted so her transmission would slow the car down, then, as they bumped down the driveway, used her hand brake so her brake lights would not be visible from the road. Now off of the Oakville Grade, she turned around at the bottom of the hill and waited, listening for the engine of the car that had been following them. She looked at the dashboard clock, following the second hand as it swept around the dial.

"What are you doing?" Paul asked, angrily, "Why are we here? He will catch us. We have nowhere to go. Why are we stopping?"

Luz held up her hand like a stop sign, then cupped it around her ear.

Paul tilted his head to one side. He nodded as the sound of screeching tires and a growling engine passed on the road just above them.

"He was catching up to us. I want him ahead of me rather than behind me," Luz said quietly.

Bowman had been approximately thirty seconds behind

her at her last look, so she waited around forty-five seconds before she slowly drove back up the hill. Had they encountered an angry homeowner during their trespass, Luz planned to share their predicament and wait there for the sheriff to come arrest them. But now she hoped to end up behind Bowman, being the hunter instead of the hunted.

Carefully exiting the driveway, Luz looked both ways on the short stretch of road visible to her from that uphill angle. With a quick rev of the engine, she pulled back onto the twisty roadway.

At some point Bowman would realize she was no longer in front of him. He would either look for somewhere to turn around, or slow down and wait for her to come up from behind him. Luz had to prepare for either eventuality.

Luz recalled hearing Christy tell Mark about a "pick" maneuver she'd learned from her stock-car-driving buddies over a Fourth of July weekend—something about tapping the car ahead of them on the left rear bumper and then passing them on the right. Apparently it worked really well if the driver in front was going into a left-hand turn.

Luz noticed the Oakville Grade was flattening out as it approached Highway 12, the road that led to Sonoma. Luz didn't want to end up in a high-speed chase on a road with lots of traffic. Bowman had already demonstrated he was willing to kill to get what he wanted, so Luz had to do what she could before he endangered other people's lives.

"Luz, I think I see brake lights up ahead," Paul said.

"Does it look like he's stopping, or do you think we've just caught up with him?"

"I don't know."

"OK, keep your seatbelt on, and be ready for impact," Luz said.

"What?!" Paul exclaimed. "Are you crazy?"

"Just hold on and do what I say. This could be rough."

As they made it around the turn, Luz saw Bowman just ahead. He was entering another left-hand turn, exactly like the one they had just driven through. Luz downshifted, then floored it, moving into the oncoming lane like she was going to pass him on the curve. Instead, she tapped him gently on the left rear bumper. The front of his car spun to the left, giving her a chance to pass him on the right. As Luz sped away, her tires screeching, she glanced in the rearview mirror and saw a smoky cloud surrounding Bowman's car. She didn't care if his left rear wheel was off the cliff and the car was teetering precariously. Bowman was a killer and all Luz wanted to do was get to a place that would be safe for her and Paul Angel.

Driving through the next curve, Luz saw the Mercedes roadster tipping towards the canyon as Bowman struggled to get the door open to get out. Then she heard a rumble like thunder and saw the car tumble down the hillside. She heard a loud boom as it exploded in red and orange flames leaving behind a plume of billowing black smoke pouring from the valley below.

Luz slowed down, "Should we stop to help him?"

"There is nothing we can do for him, poor man," Paul said, as he crossed himself and said a silent blessing . "God has dealt with him in his own way."

"I guess the danger is over," Luz said, quietly.

"Who knows?" Paul responded. Luz nodded her head somberly. "Let's go."

Up ahead she could see Highway 12, which would lead her to the heart of Sonoma and to the raceway. When she arrived at the intersection, she took a deep breath then made a left turn toward town.

Once she'd made it through the city streets and could put on some speed, Luz floored it. Two patrol cars going in the opposite direction raced passed her driving toward the Oakville Grade to the site of Fred Bowman's fiery crash. Following those two emergency vehicles were two firetrucks and an ambulance.

Luz passed through the intersection with Highway 121. Now the speedway property was on her right side. She made a quick right turn into the Gate One entrance, where most of the competitors entered the track, then drove to the paddock parking area, flashing her pass and credentials at the security official. Behind her, at just that moment, Sacha Bernard's white Bentley convertible turned into the same entrance, its horn blaring. When Luz stopped the car, Sacha ran up to Paul Angel, leaving the motor running on the Bentley and gave him a big hug. He was crying. "Paul, *mon ami*! It is you! You are safe!"

Turning to Luz, he gave her the same hug and a kiss on each cheek. "You've saved my friend's life, and Chateau La Mer. It is a marvelous day!"

CHAPTER 24

Shaken by the harrowing drive through the mountains, shocked by the explosive crash of the Mercedes resulting in Bowman's death, Luz leaned her head against the steering wheel of the car and collected her thoughts.

She unintentionally caused the death of another human being while defending her life and that of Paul Angel. Had she not driven like her life depended on it, would she and Paul be dead now? She felt remorse, anger, and the desire to know the truth. Were others behind the death of Orval Slattery, and if so, who were they?

Sacha had escorted Paul away to some other part of the paddock area. Luz only hoped they were no longer in danger. As she'd learned at Indy, anything could happen in the middle of a race track, even murder.

As she walked toward the garages, noticing that most of the cars were setting up on the grid, Luz knew she had very little time before the race started. Stopping in the rest room, when she looked in the mirror, Luz was horrified by what she saw reflected back at her.

Scrapes on her face, dirt on her cheeks, her hair matted and unkempt. She washed her face, used her finger to brush her teeth, and French braided her hair. No amount of makeup was going to cover up what she'd been through in the last 48 hours, so all she did was gloss her lips and bravely smiled as she walked out the door to face whatever awaited her in the pits.

Fortunately, when she went to the transporter, there was a team hat waiting for her and she found an old pair of sunglasses to hide her weary eyes and the circles under them. Once on the pit road, she looked toward the Amberson-Harwood scoring stand where Sacha, Paul, Sara, Michelle, and Clint were hugging and laughing, joyously celebrating the rescue and escape from Chateau La Mer.

Looking down to the Blackbird pit box, Luz saw Girard Morel and his girlfriend in serious conversation with Roger Schneider. For just having met this week, they certainly seemed chummy. How did they know one another? And how was Schneider involved?

Lost in thought, Luz turned to walk to the Amberson-Harwood pit box. Most of the team was out on the grid for the start of the race and the send-off of the two cars. Waiting at the scoring stand for her was Detective Travis Boone.

"Good morning, Ms. Dane. It sounds like you have been living a very exciting life since I last saw you," the detective said sarcastically.

"Oh, I don't know. Being kidnapped, escaping from imprisonment, racing through the mountains…" Luz said casually, and then as she started to say more, she covered her face and broke into sobs.

Taking her into his arms and holding her, Travis Boone said, "I know you've been through a lot. Too much probably. And if you are upset about the accident, you didn't kill him. He killed himself. Take a few deep breaths, and here, drink a few sips of water."

They stepped apart and he handed her a bottle of water. Slightly embarrassed about her outburst, Luz dried her tears with the handkerchief he gave her, and quenched her thirst. Puzzled by how comforted she felt by this man she only knew from his job in law enforcement, Luz couldn't think of a thing to say.

"Later today, I'm going to meet with local law enforcement for a conference call with Martin Cohen, my department, and the partners of Chateau La Mer. We'll wrap things up then. Meanwhile your team has a race to run," Boone said.

Surprised, Luz said, "What happened to the detective I met in San Antonio? You sure are relaxed compared to the last time I saw you."

"As you know, a lot has happened in these two weeks. I know and understand a lot more than before. Look, the race is about to start. You have things to do, so take your place with your team, and know I'll be right here watching over things until it is all over." Detective Boone, smiled pleasantly at Luz, and helped her up to her seat on the scoring stand as he slid in next to her.

CHAPTER 25

From her seat on top of the scoring stand, Luz looked out over the track, where she could see the grassy brown hillsides dotted with people, the S-curves of the carousel, and the grid with the cars lined up two by two, with team members in their livery surrounding each vehicle.

There was concern about the remaining partners' safety until more information was available about how many other people besides Fred Bowman were involved in taking over Chateau La Mer which explained the presence of Detective Travis Boone.

Paul, now wearing a gimme-cap and sunglasses, could easily have passed for a sponsor or a friend of the Ambersons. She could hear a murmur of conversation between Paul and Sara behind her, though they were not loud enough for her to distinguish any words.

When the "start engines" call was made, Luz noticed Roger

Schneider, wearing a nondescript fire suit—one that looked remarkably like that of a sanctioning body official—lurking off to one side of the grid, nowhere near the yellow Blackbird Racing car. He was holding something in his hand. What was it? She focused her binoculars on him as he ran alongside the race cars now pulling forward on the warm-up lap. What was he doing? Frantically she scanned the grid, the moving cars, and the pit road looking for him, but he seemed to have disappeared into thin air.

At Indy, Roger had sabotaged their car during the pit stop competition by turning off the source of compressed air needed to operate the wheel guns. When the team went to change the tires, nothing happened, and Roger's team ran away with the $100,000 prize. He managed to thwart their effort with such a tiny detail, one the team should have checked ahead of time. Now Luz wondered if he was employing another simple yet undetectable means to make sure his team did well—well enough to be considered for a Formula International audition with Sacha Bernard's team. It was no secret to anyone in the garage area that Sacha Bernard was scouting for his next Formula International driver.

Since she'd lost so much time being kidnapped and imprisoned at Chateau La Mer, Luz didn't know what to expect for this race, which had such long lap times. She reviewed the practice statistics and qualifying numbers, and watched the digital map showing each car's placement on the track. She kept wondering what Schneider might be doing on the grid, though she felt helpless to do anything about it. Luz sighed as she watched the cars make their way around the undulating track through the Sonoma hills.

After the warm-up lap, the field re-formed for the race in the order determined by their qualifying times. Christi and Mark had qualified in the first and second slots. Blackbird's Matt Locke was lined up fourth, right behind Mark. When the green flag waved, the cars shot straight uphill toward turn 1, going to the right, then followed the track to where it flattened out and went downhill to the left. There, as they wound their way through the S-curves, Christi's right rear tire slid off the tarmac onto the dirt, and she began to slide downhill. She corrected, barely missing Matt Locke, who passed her teammate and was pushing forward to take first position.

"I think my right rear is losing air, maybe flat," Christi barked into her headset.

"OK, pit this time around," Jeff said. "We'll just have to fight our way through the pack once you are back out there." Luz could hear the disappointment in his voice.

All of the team members got in position, waiting for Christi to come in so they could change her tires and top off the fuel. Mark stayed out. He had slipped back to a middle position but was making every effort to defend his place in the lineup.

Smoothly Christie drove into the pit box, the team serviced the car, and she sped away, sliding into sixth place as she rejoined the pack.

After the pit stop, their tire guy, Tommy James, carefully examined all four tires, smoothing his hands along their surface and then checking how each one sat on its rim. He motioned to Jeff to come look at the one that had been on the right rear. "Look at this, will you?"

Jeff took a close look at the spot Tommy pointed out to him, even pulling a flashlight out of his toolbox.

"Does that look like a puncture to you?" Tommy asked.

"Yeah, it is a really clean hole," Jeff said. "Like it was made with an ice pick or a knife, not like it was from a piece of debris in the marbles on the side of the track."

Luz overheard them and thought about Roger. Could that have been an ice pick in his hand, or was she imagining things? In any case, there was no way to prove it or protest it or do anything to change the outcome of the race: there was a lot more time left before it was over.

The representative of the tire company providing their tires for the Sonoma race came to check the wear of the set they'd just changed. Tommy James pointed out the hole, but the two of them shrugged, not sure what might have caused it.

As the race progressed, more teams came in with tire problems, to the point where the announcers started to speculate on whether the compound was somehow defective or the wrong tires had been brought to the track. Each time a car came in for a change due to a sudden or even gradual deflation, the tire representative checked the tires' condition and attempted to document the degradation of the compound. After twenty laps—basically one-quarter of the race—twenty cars had been in for tire service, and only a few were still on their first set of tires. Matt Locke of Blackbird Racing was in the lead.

Luz was still keeping track of Christi and Mark's lap times. She was also noting when the other teams' cars were in for a tire change and how it affected the overall points and positions for the championship.

Luz motioned Tommy James over to the scoring stand. "Is it my imagination, or are there are lot of tire problems in a short amount of time for this race?"

"It sure seems that way," he said. "Let me see what the tire rep says now that we are further into the race, and I'll check in with a few of my friends on other teams. I'll let you know what I find out."

"Great! It seems so odd that over half the field has been in the pits with tire problems before the first half of the race," Luz said, and he nodded in agreement. She patted Tommy on the back before he walked down the pit road in search of his cohorts on other teams.

Watching him walk away, Luz noticed that one of the race officials was in the Blackbird pit area talking to Blake Notzen, a Blackbird team member. Something was off—the uniform was a bit snug, or the pant legs was too long—and that called attention to the person wearing it. Studying him through her binoculars, Luz gasped: it was Roger Schneider. What was he doing wearing a race official uniform? So she hadn't imagined what she had seen earlier. He really was impersonating an official: he was still wearing a fire suit, just as he had when he was on the grid at the start of the race.

It was about time for Christi and Mark to pass by and begin yet another lap. Luz noted their lap times when they whizzed by and then looked toward the Blackbird pits again. Roger had disappeared.

Looking down the pit alley, Luz saw Tommy James and the tire rep in a heated discussion. Another couple of team members, all wearing different livery, were part of the group. Each one was showing photos to the others and notebooks where they seemed to be comparing data. The tire rep did not look happy, and was doing his best to calm down those in front of him. With most of the field on the far side of the track, Luz could hear what he was saying.

"Look, I know it's not our tire compound. And from the photos you've shown me, and the tires I've looked at, and the data you've kept, it sure looks like almost the whole field was sabotaged, but I can't prove it."

After listening to more grumbling from the team members surrounding him, the tire rep said, "OK, I'll go talk to the race officials and maybe we can get this looked into, but I can tell you it probably won't make a difference in how this race turns out today, unless they can figure out who's behind it, and then penalize them after the fact."

Luz could not believe her eyes as Roger Schneider, wearing the race official's uniform, walked right up to the group and demanded that they clear the walkway behind the pit stalls, reminding them that it needed to be open in the event of a fire emergency. With his sunglasses on and an official's gimme-cap, Roger successfully passed himself off as one of the race stewards. Quickly Luz took a picture of him as he turned her way, then she watched him walk away, hoping he'd be back in his official capacity and she could get another, better photo.

It was obvious to Luz that Roger was behind the sabotage of all the cars. How easily he could have created slow leaks in just one tire as he passed by on the grid, claiming he was just doing an inspection of the car, impersonating a race official, checking any number of things on the cars before the start. A slow leak on a tire wouldn't be nearly as dangerous as creating an oil leak, or disabling the brakes or the suspension. But what did he have to gain by so obviously affecting so many cars?

As she stared out over the track, waiting for Mark and Christi to come back by the front straightaway, Luz heard Jeff's voice. "This should be the last pit stop, I hope. Everyone get ready. Let's execute this one flawlessly. I want all the tires on and the car full of fuel before it's released. Christi is coming in first, and then Mark after her." His voice sounded tense and commanding.

Christi made it in and the crew performed as expected. She was in and out without a hitch. Mark took over the first-place spot and stayed out of trouble during his lap as the leader. When it was his turn in the pits, the crew gave him the same fast service and made sure he was released so he could blend in with the pack right behind Christi, who was running second.

As they made their way through the twists and turns of the carousel, Christi sailed through turn 6, easily exiting it for a strong run on the back section of the track. Mark ran into traffic of a few lapped cars that slowed him down coming off turn 5 going into the blind corner at turn 6. As he tried to make it through the turn, a few cars passed him, pushing him back to fourth place as he worked his way through the road course. Matt Locke was driving one of the cars that passed Mark, making up for lost time behind the tumble of cars stuck trying to get through the series of turns.

As Luz was keeping up with the lap times and the cars' positions on the track, she tried to catch Jeff's eye. He ignored her efforts to get his attention. Instead he focused on the images from the closed-circuit camera feed showing the parts of the track up in the hills away from the pit road.

With only a few more laps to go, Jeff noticed a team official hovering around their scoring stand, trying to get Sacha Bernard's attention. It was odd for the officials to be roaming around the pit row when there were no cars in the pits. Jeff took a closer look at the uniform, hat, and sunglasses, and the fit of the fire suit. Something just wasn't right about the whole get-up. And why would he want to talk with Sacha Bernard? Sacha was a guest for this open-wheel race—an important guest, to be sure, but not a team owner or official.

"Can I help you?" Jeff straightened up his six-foot two-inch frame as he asked this question.

"I wanted to talk to Mr. Bernard," said the official, who sounded a lot like Roger Schneider.

"Roger? Roger Schneider? Is this Halloween? Why are you all dressed up like a race official? Are you impersonating a race official? Why aren't you paying attention to this race? Matt is doing a great job for you! He's running second behind my driver, Christi Cole!"

Roger looked up at Jeff, then turned around and walked briskly back to the Blackbird pit box. As he left, Jeff was approached by Giselle Mouton, who had been standing nearby, waiting.

"An interview with you after the race?" she asked.

"Of course," he said. "Anything for you, Giselle. But first we have to finish the race."

Luz overheard their conversation and sighed. It wasn't her fault that she was locked in a cellar overnight and didn't make the Calcutta party. She focused on the track and the final two laps, and decided that after all she had been through, she just wanted to get back to the hotel and go to sleep after the race was over. No celebrations. No interviews. No men. Jeff could have all the French models he wanted, and she'd work on her own life plan with or without him.

Right after the cars started on the last lap, with Christi in first, Matt Locke in second, and Mark Miller running third, Jeff came up to Luz. "We're going to file a protest against Roger Schneider. I want you to write it up. There are four other teams that want to be part of it. Tommy James can give you their names. We need to get it into the stewards within thirty minutes of the race finishing. I think you can use a computer and printer in the press center. Go now!"

Luz looked at him. "What are you protesting? Do you have a rulebook? Don't I have to pick out a section of the rulebook to base the protest on?"

Jeff scowled at her. He pulled a worn and dog-eared copy of the rulebook out of his back pocket. Flipping through it, he found a page with a turned-down corner, and showed it to her, pointing his finger at a section he'd circled earlier when he was talking with the tire rep and other team owners. It was a section relating to sabotage, and as Luz read it, Tommy James handed her a list of teams and their owners to include in the protest.

"I need you to go now. Type it up, find those owners, get

them to sign it, and then bring it to me. I hope to be on the podium with my drivers. That is when I'll hand it to the race steward. He should be right there with me. Quick! Go!"

Luz climbed down from the scoring stand and ran through the garage area crowd, trying to remember where the press-room was. She saw a sign and found the door, walking into an eerily quiet room: everyone was mesmerized by the final lap.

Sitting down at a computer over in the corner away from most of the people in the room, she started to type away, creating a protest that followed the wording stipulated in the rule-book. As she wrote it out off the top of her head, she made sure that she mentioned not only the specific section Jeff had given her, but any other she could think of that might be applicable. The basis of the protest was that Roger Schneider had used an ice pick to create leaks in tires—an act that could have endangered the lives of all the drivers, plus anyone in the pits and spectators in the stands. She finished it up with signature blocks for all of the five teams that wanted to sign it. With many teams fielding multiple entries, over half the field was affected and was making the allegations and filing the protest. Quickly checking spelling and grammar, Luz printed eight copies of the protest: one for each team, the steward, and a few extras in case they were needed.

She collected the copies and made sure each one was legible, then she deleted the file on the computer in the press-room. She ran back to the pit road, arriving just as the cars were returning to the pits, and looked for the owners needed to sign the protest.

Still not knowing how the race had turned out, tired from

her ordeal at Chateau La Mer, and rushing to complete the protest so that Jeff could hand it to the steward within the thirty-minute time span, Luz was starting to feel lightheaded and slightly confused. She'd consumed that one energy bar hours before, at the beginning of the chase through the mountains. Now she couldn't slow down—she didn't have time to waste.

Turning to the left onto pit row, Luz looked down the long walkway and figured out the fastest way to get to the team owners she needed to contact. Dodging a tire cart and managing to avoid bumping into a fire marshal, she made it all the way to the farthest end of the row. There she encountered the first person to sign, and then she went from one to another, all the while assuring them she would return a completed copy to each one of them. Having them sign eight copies of the same document took a while for most of them, along with the conversation about how awful it was to have to file the protest in the first place. Luz moved assuredly through the crowd. But just as she arrived at the podium and winner's circle to meet Jeff, she bumped into Roger Schneider.

"Hey, look where you're going!" he yelled. "Just because your team won again doesn't give you license to knock into other people. I should file assault charges against you, you little bitch."

Grabbing her wrist, Schneider tried to drag her in the opposite direction, and Luz did her best to resist, shrieking as loud as she could. "Let go of me! Stop it! I didn't mean to run into you. Believe me. Let me go!"

The crowd at the Winner's Circle turned in their direction to see what was going on. At that moment, a security official appeared. "Sir, please let go of this lady's wrist. Right now. If you don't, I will arrest you."

Schneider raised his arm and let Luz's wrist drop out of his hand, in a show of sarcastic obedience. The official motioned to Luz to leave, and she hopped over the pit wall and ran to the stage, where the team was posing for a photo, each wearing the latest sponsor's hat. As she placed the new blue hat on her head, she shoved the protest papers into Jeff's hand. "Sign all of these, please, when we're done with the photos. You don't have much time left to get this to the steward. The other copies are for the other team owners."

With a couple more hat changes, the group started to disband, and Jeff signed the protest forms. He handed all but one back to Luz, who left the stage to find the other owners and distribute the documents.

When the chief steward approached Jeff to congratulate the team on their win, Jeff handed him the protest. "A group of us think this deserves some action on the part of the race stewards. Hope it doesn't ruin the afternoon for you."

Watching him from the pit road was Giselle, who was waiting for her interview. When Jeff stepped down from the presentation stage, she came up to him and gave him a big kiss as she took a selfie of the two of them. She started her camera going and began the interview, alternately flirting with him and asking him sharp questions about the race and strategy needed to win on a road course.

When Luz returned from running around delivering the protests, she walked back to where most of the team crowded around Christi and Mark, both holding up their trophies, only to see Giselle whispering in Jeff's ear, her arm wrapped around his waist, and his around hers. They looked very cozy together.

It stopped Luz in her tracks. Suddenly she felt exhausted. Turning around, she headed to the scoring stand to pick up anything she might have left there, running into Travis Boone when she did.

"You look all tuckered out, Ms. Dane. Are you ready to help us finish this murder case?" the detective asked her, his eyes twinkling. She'd forgotten about the meeting he'd mentioned. One more thing to add to what was turning out to be an extremely painful day.

"Sure, want a ride?" She asked.

"I've got my own car right over here." He said, pointing to a beige SUV near the exit to the paddock. " Why don't you follow me?"

"Got it." Luz said, as the two of them then walked out to the parking lot to their cars.

She didn't see Sacha or Clint or Michelle or Sara or Paul. Goodness knew where they were—probably celebrating somewhere. Luz felt anything but celebratory at that moment.

Slipping into the seat of the red BMW, she started the engine, took the top down, drank the last inch of water in the bottle from earlier in the day, and followed Detective Boone to the police station in Sonoma.

BARBIE O'CONNOR

CHAPTER 26

Driving away, Luz felt the wind in her hair. Taking the top down on a convertible always gave her a sensation of freedom. The last twenty-four hours she'd lived through—the hours since she had woken up in the grimy closet with Paul Angel as her guide and protector—felt like a month.

The fields of grass and the hillsides covered in grape vines heavy with ripe fruit barely registered with her as she drove back through the farm roads cluttered with cars that had left the racetrack. Normally Luz would notice the beauty of nature contrasting starkly with man's harsh intrusion into an area, but today she was dealing with her loneliness and her wounded pride.

She'd left the firm where she'd grown up as a woman and a professional and started her own firm with the intention to have the freedom to have it all. She wanted a man, a profession, and a family, whether it was a race team or a brood of her own, and now she felt she'd given up everything for an illusion, for a dream that could not possibly come true.

The image of Giselle and Jeff laughing together at the track, their bodies intertwined, pierced her heart. She should have been in his arms, she should have been by his side, but where was she? In a grubby hole in the ground trying to solve a mystery to help one of her clients hold on to a family business. Writing a multipage protest and getting five different team owners to sign it in a tiny sliver of time so it could be filed with the chief steward. She was always helping other people have the best life they could. What a mistake! She was a failure in her own life; how could she help others with theirs?

It had been a long time since Luz had beaten herself up with her own thoughts and self-talk. Her mood sank lower with each mile she drove, and she almost didn't notice when the detective turned into the parking lot of the Sonoma police facility.

So tired, she followed him into the police station. Walking through the maze of hallways to a small conference room, Luz thought about all the facts she knew and the details that were still loose ends. Once she was seated at the table, with a note pad in front of her, pencil in hand, Luz doodled and drew diagrams linking the facts together.

In the next few moments, Paul Angel, Sacha Bernard, and Sara Slattery entered the room and sat down next to Luz. Then Girard Morel, Roger Schneider, and Giselle Mouton were escorted in and seated on the opposite side of the table as the others. Detective Boone joined the group along with a court reporter, an administrative assistant and two Sonoma

County sheriff deputies.

Detective Boone instructed his assistant to conference Martin Cohen on the screen located at the other end of the table so he could be part of the meeting. Then he dictated to the court reporter the date, time, and the names of all who were present at the meeting. He reminded all those present of their Miranda rights. On hearing that, Luz raised her eyebrows as she looked around the table at the others who were present realizing that one or more of them were responsible for the murder of Orval Slattery.

"Let's start with the facts about the night Orval Slattery died," Boone began, "The wine Orval drank was poisoned with ethyl alcohol. Just recently we determined that it was in the presentation bottles of wine, the magnums supposedly packed for him by Paul Angel." Everyone in the room stared at the wizened old man who looked like an elf.

"But Mr. Angel's fingerprints were not found on the bottles. There were other prints found on the bottles." Sacha Bernard sighed with relief, patting the hand of his old friend and partner.

Luz was listening, but at the same time thinking about the significance of Girard, Giselle, and Roger being in the meeting. She glanced over at them, studying their faces, and looking at their hands.

"Although Fred Bowman, alias Frederick Le Beaux, and his wife, Maurine Henry, were employed for many years at Chateau La Mer, neither of their prints were found on either of the bottles. Yet, both of their fingerprints were found on the phony codicil sent to Martin Cohen's office the day Orval died. Mr.

Slattery's were not." Boone stated.

Luz pondered what she'd just heard. She jotted down a few notes, crossed out a few lines, and then circled one of the names on her pad.

Luz then said, "Is anyone thirsty? It was a hot day at the track." Paul Angel nodded his head, as did Detective Boone.

She poured several glasses of water from the pitcher on the table, handing them to those seated around the table.

Noticing that Girard kept looking at his watch, Luz turned to him and said, "I know you are a busy man, and want to get out of here, but a little cool water might be good before you rush off. After all, you spent all day at the track. You must be thirsty." She poured him a glass of water and handed it to him.

"I don't want water. I want to leave." Girard said. Annoyed, he grabbed the glass, took a sip and then placed it back on the table. "You can't keep me here. You don't have any evidence that I was involved in that murder."

Luz smiled, as she watched one of the deputies pick up the glass and open the door to leave the room. While he could hear him, Detective Boone spoke up, saying, "You know what to do." The deputy nodded and closed the door.

Absorbed with his own tirade, Girard Morel stood up from the table and said, "Look, I don't know why I am here. I'm a busy man and I have a plane to catch."

Girard moved toward the door and said, "Giselle, I'm not staying here any longer. It is time to leave. Let's go."

Giselle rose from the table, moving closer to Girard, putting her arm through his. Together they walked toward the doorway.

Blocking their exit was Detective Boone, who asked, "What is your hurry, Girard? Giselle?"

There was a knock on the door. Boone heard his deputy say, "Open the door. We found a match on the prints."

"Will do. Watch it. I've got two who are ready to bolt."

Opening the door, Boone took the sheet of paper passed to him, and Girard lunged for it, pushing Giselle between Boone and the deputy. Girard grabbed the door knob and pulled, pushing Giselle toward the open door.

Luz jumped up from the table and grabbed Giselle by the shoulders, pulling her away from the exit. Off balance, the two women fell to the floor.

"Let go of me!" Giselle screamed, as she cartwheeled her arms working to push Luz away and get up off the floor. To keep Girard from leaving, Luz scooted right behind him and kicked her leg out hitting him behind the knee. The blow knocked him down and he collapsed on the floor. Detective Boone knelt down putting pressure on Girard's shoulders and quickly handcuffed him. He pulled him off the floor, and pushed him into one of the conference room chairs.

"Ms. Mouton, please take a seat. Until I get answers to a few questions, you are not going anywhere," Boone said to her as he pulled out a chair for her.

Furious, Girard yelled, "Now that Bowman is dead, you can't prove anything."

"Frederick!" Giselle yelled out, "It was all Frederick's idea. And you, you murdered him." Pointing her finger at Luz, Giselle burst into tears.

Luz looked down at the table, and then looking at Giselle,

shook off the accusation by saying, "Bowman knocked me out, incarcerated me and did the same to Paul Angel. When we escaped from his prison, he chased us down the Oakville Grade with the intent to kill us. He killed himself by driving off the side of the cliff."

"Girard knew how to do things. They were boys together. And Roger, he is a client of Girard's and I help his race driver, Matt. We have done nothing wrong." Giselle said.

"Giselle, you know all about Girard, since you've known each other since you were teenagers. You both changed your names and your identities when you came to America. Girard adopted the persona of a wealthy financier and while running his bucket shop got lucky with a few IPOs that made him money for a while," Luz said.

"I know about that. Girard sold me a stock that made me millions." Schneider said.

"And did he promise you millions from the Chateau La Mer deal too? Or were you hoping for sponsorship money that you were promised when Girard and Frederick planned to take over the company after Orval's death?" Luz baited him.

Schneider in a fit of anger said, "They promised me there would be money. Money from the investment and money from sponsorship. You know how much it costs to run one of these teams. I can't keep up."

"Shut up Roger!" Morel yelled, "You stupid fool. We'll all end up in jail."

Luz raised her eyebrows and while looking directly at Giselle, said, "Giselle is just arm candy. I'm sure she can do better than you. Is that why you did it? So you could keep up with her lifestyle?"

A torrent of French profanity spewed from Giselle's mouth, as she stood up angrily and shook her fist at Luz. "Girard has done nothing wrong. He was helping a friend that is all!"

"So which friend was he helping? Bowman or Schneider?" Luz asked, coyly.

Girard gave her a murderous look. Carefully, Giselle said, "Girard only talked about the IPO. I think he's being framed."

"Just the same, we're going to take your prints before you leave today and check for any matches that might exist." He ushered in another deputy who took custody of them.

On returning to the conference room, he said, "Luz, would you like to tell Sara the whole story?" Detective Boone asked.

Luz nodded her head, and began, "Girard Morel first approached Orval Slattery about buying his shares several years ago, but he was rebuffed. Then he spoke with Paul Angel, who also refused him. But Girard knew something about Paul Angel—he knew what he did in the Resistance, because he was the last remaining member of the LeBeaux family."

There was a gasp from Sacha, who said, "But Frederick, was he not the grandson? The last surviving member of the LeBeaux family?"

"No Sacha, Fred Bowman was an orphan, like Paul. He was best friends with Girard LeBeaux who was the grandson. Frederick was raised by the grandfather along with his grandson. Both boys changed their names when they came to America. And both boys grew up to hate the owners of Chateau Bernard and subsequently, the owners of Chateau La Mer,"

Luz stated.

"Sara, your grandfather was killed by two greedy men who wanted revenge, money and power," Detective Boone interjected, then continued, "They copied Paul Angel's technique for poisoning the wine. Morel and Bowman planned for Paul to take the blame for Orval's death. Bowman forged Orval's signature on the codicil, and Morel forged Paul Angel's on the stock certificates and on the letter he left for you and the note for Orval that was left in his office with the intent that you would find it."

Travis Boone held out the sheet of paper brought to him earlier by the deputy, "The prints check out—Morel is wanted for forgeries all over the world. And most importantly, they match the ones on the magnum wine bottle from the charity dinner where Orval Slattery died. As a winemaker, Bowman knew how to create the elixir of death to be added to the wine, but Morel's prints leave us no doubt he was the one who actually added the poison to the bottle of wine."

Boone handed Sara the silver perfume atomizer, saying, "I am sorry you lost your grandfather through the acts of these very selfish and greedy men. Luz shared with me the intended purpose of this little bottle and its contents. Lucky for you, only your grandfather's prints were on the glass vial holding what was a quick acting mixture of almond liquor and arsenic. If I were you, I'd destroy it. I already removed the contents. You are in the clear."

"Sara, now that we have proof that the codicil naming Paul Angel as trustee was a forgery, the original will executed by your grandfather is in effect," Martin Cohen said from the screen. "Congratulations Miss Slattery, you now control one-third of Chateau La Mer winery. I wish you a long and very successful tenure as one of the three owners of one of the greatest wineries in the world!"

"You two gentlemen are lucky to be alive. Paul, you have Luz to thank for your rescue. Although it sounds like you had a wild ride to freedom." Boone said, then added, "And Sacha, this afternoon at the track the Sonoma County sheriff's department bomb squad found an explosive device attached to your Bentley. It was carefully disarmed and removed during the race."

Wide eyed in horror, Sacha at first was speechless, then he humbly said, "Detective Boone, I am so grateful. So grateful to be alive."

Boone laughed, "It's all in a day's work for those of us in law enforcement. Safety first. We had to consider every possible way you could "accidentally" die and work as fast as possible to counteract whatever we found," Boone said, then added, "I think that for now the three of you can move on with your lives as you wish."

Sara, Sacha and Paul shook hands with Boone and the two deputies as they left the room. Luz stood up, and started for the door.

"No, no, no. Not you. Not yet," Detective Boone said. "There are a couple of things I want to say to you. First, thanks for tripping Morel when he was attempting to escape."

"You would have done the same for me," Luz said, impatiently, stretching her neck, as she moved to the door.

"And second, earlier at the track, when you broke down,

I felt you really needed someone to hold you and let you cry and release all that emotion you were feeling after all you'd been through. I may have been out of line and I want to apologize to you if I offended you in any way. Please forgive me," Boone said, extending his hand out to her.

Luz was taken aback by his forthright concern, and shook hands with him. "I'll forgive you. But I'm surprised by how differently you are treating me now, so differently than when you first started on the case. What happened?"

"Yes, well, about that. I didn't know anything about you except that you were at a fancy-dress ball where a murder took place and you had your own business and had clients with a lot of money. And you weren't afraid of me. I learned more about you as I worked the case and talked to various people. You've worked for everything you have from what I hear and you are as smart as they come. In fact, after this case is wrapped up, would it be alright if I called you? To go out?" Boone said, carefully.

"Ummm, are you sure?" Luz said, hesitantly, "I'm okay with it, but I've been told dating me can be challenging."

"Yes, I can imagine. Then I'll call you sometime. Tonight you've got a lot to celebrate. Enjoy it all!" Boone said, as he walked her to her car.

Luz got into the little red convertible, drove a few blocks and was surprised when she almost missed the turnoff for the inn where she was staying. She was distracted about Detective Boone and wondered if he was serious about calling her?

By the time she reached the valet parking stand, her exhaustion took over and Luz felt tired and worn out. Barely able to smile as Robbie greeted her, she handed him the keys as she slid out of the car.

"Ms. Dane, are you feeling alright?" the young valet asked as he helped her up out of the sports car.

Luz leaned back against the car, her face pale. She took a few deep breaths.

"I'm just really tired." Luz walked slowly up the stairs into the lobby and toward the elevator, feeling overwhelmed.

Luz managed to reach her room and open the door with the key she finally found after rummaging through her bag, and let the door close shut behind her. Taking off her clothes, she let them drop to the floor and turned the shower on. She guzzled a full bottle of water that was sitting on the counter, then stepped into the warm shower and lathered all the grime and dirt off her body and out of her hair. After drying off, she made her way to the bed, crept under the covers, and, as soon as her head hit the pillow, fell asleep.

BARBIE O'CONNOR

CHAPTER 27

Sleeping hard, Luz was deep into a dream about an underground cave when someone knocked at the door. Thinking it was part of her dream, something about a miner wielding his pickax looking for gold, Luz ignored the sound, snuggling further into her pillows. With each knock she tried to return to her dream, working to remember where she was.

A moment later, she heard a familiar voice, and the voice and the tapping sound got louder. "Luz! Luz, wake up!"

It was Jeff. At first he cajoled her, then his tone grew firmer. "Come on, Luz, you can't ignore me forever. I'm not going away until you get up and let me in."

She pulled the pillow over her ears and burrowed into the feather comforter, keeping her eyes closed. Even with all the attempts at soundproofing, she could still hear him say, "Look, Luz, I know you are angry with me and think the worst of me, but please give me a chance to talk to you. Please, Luz."

What was Jeff doing banging on her door? He was all cozy with that reporter, Giselle, when she last saw him. Now what did he want?

Luz sat up and scowled at her reflection in the mirror. All her hair was springing around her head like a lion's mane. Her face had crease marks from the pillows, her eyes were swollen, and her head ached. Would Jeff ever stop banging on the door?

She pulled on a bathrobe and took a swig of water from the glass on the bedside table, swishing it around in her mouth to get rid of that cottony feeling. Then she took a deep breath and said, "Hold your horses, I'm coming."

Opening the door with her left hand, and with her right hand on her hip, Luz surveyed Jeff from head to toe and waited for him to say something.

He was wearing a tuxedo; his hair was dried into stylish waves as if he'd made an effort to mimic the actor playing James Bond in the latest 007 movie. In one hand he held a vase filled with a bouquet of a dozen yellow roses, and in the other a chilled bottle of champagne with two flutes. The roses looked a little shell-shocked from all the banging on the door, but Luz didn't care. Her eyes were a steely gray-blue as she waved Jeff into her room. Still not saying a word, she closed the door, walked over to the small round café table by the balcony door, and sat down.

At first Jeff sat on the bed, but he soon joined Luz at the table, where he placed one flute in front of her and the other near himself. Luckily the flowers were already in a vase, which he placed on the café table. Luz was still silent: she had decided to wait to hear what excuse Jeff would invent to appease her. She was the one who in the past had apologized for her inability to "be there" for him, or her inability to accommodate his schedule. She had never dated anyone else since they started to see each other, and she had never been intimate with another man while she was linked with Jeff, so her apologies were about her career or her responsibilities to her clients or to her closest friends. Her excuses were all about helping other people rather than pleasing herself. This was a new challenge for their relationship, since it involved another woman, Giselle. Was Luz a priority for Jeff anymore, or just another woman who was conveniently available for him to dally with when it suited him?

Jeff poured them each a glass of champagne, and raised his glass to her. She answered with her own flute, lightly touching his with hers. He put his other hand over hers, then made the toast: "To our Formula International chance."

Luz questioned him with her eyes, took a sip of the toasty, bubbling wine, and set her glass down. She pushed her chair back and tilted her head to one side. She did not want to fight about Giselle, nor did she want to give up on their relationship. Luz was still tired from her ordeal over the last two days, and she was still processing the events of the past week: the attempted takeover of Chateau La Mer, the fiery death of Fred Bowman, Roger Schneider sabotaging cars in hopes of winning a chance at a FIR team and Orval Slattery's murder.

All she wanted to do at that moment was get back in bed, think about who was responsible for what, and make sure that the people she loved and cared about were safe and their futures were secure.

"Luz, are you listening to me? It's six-thirty, and dinner is at seven. You need to get ready."

Pulled out of her reverie, Luz shook her head. "I'm not going, Jeff." She stood up and moved toward the door, and Jeff followed.

"Luz, I'm sorry. I was an idiot. You didn't show up for the Calcutta party. You didn't answer your phone. I never got a message from you or a text. I thought you'd dumped me for that investment banker, Girard Morel." Jeff looked sheepish.

Luz leaned up against the dresser and shook her head. "I've never given you cause to suspect that I would dump you for another man. Sure, I've been late for dates, unable to make a trip or two to a race track when you asked me to join you, and occasionally had to dash away early from lunch with you because I had to take care of business for my clients, but I am not going to apologize for any of my actions. I've only been doing what a responsible, competent woman does."

She sighed, then continued. "So if you think I'm going to grovel and say I'm sorry, forget about it. That's not happening. I just managed to solve one murder and prevent another, as well as save my own life and Paul Angel's too. Plus I coached the real owners of Chateau La Mer how to avoid a hostile takeover of their very important Franco-American winery, all while helping a client who happens to be a friend of mine. If you'd rather date that selfie stick of a French reporter who doubles as Girard Morel's girlfriend, then be my guest. I hope you two are very happy together." Luz opened the door to her room and, with a flourish, waved her arm to indicate that Jeff could leave.

Just as the door opened, Michelle rustled down the hall in a taffeta cocktail dress and glanced into the room. She did a double-take, then stopped and bustled into the room. "Luz, you aren't ready! The limo will be here in a few minutes. Let me help you get dressed," she said. "Jeff, be a nice boy and go down to the lobby and let Clint know Luz and I will be there in a jiffy."

Jeff followed her instructions and quietly closed the door, leaving Michelle and Luz alone. Placing her crystal-covered evening bag on the café table, Michelle noticed the yellow roses and the two flutes, one empty and the other just barely touched. She'd seen Luz leaving the track by herself, seen her swinging out of the parking lot in the red convertible with her dark hair caught by the wind. Nothing like the feeling of hair flowing freely in a convertible to improve one's mood, Michelle had thought at the time. She knew Luz was hurt by what she had seen at the track and how Jeff had treated her, but she also knew that the two of them loved each other, so she'd have to do whatever she could to help them get back in each other's arms.

Michelle walking over to the closet, looked through the dresses hanging there, and pulled out one she hoped would work for tonight's celebration. Digging through the drawers nearby, she found the right underclothes, a purse, and a small jewelry roll, and laid them out on the bed.

"Luz, I know that boy hurt your feelings, but remember, you came here this weekend to work for Amberson-Harwood Racing and to help your client Sara out of a jam. We have a lot to celebrate tonight: we won the race, and the winery has been saved, and Paul Angel is still alive." Michelle spoke in a soothing tone as she rubbed Luz's shoulder. "So put on your makeup, get dressed, and let's go enjoy the evening."

Luz didn't want to disappoint her dear friend, so she did as she was asked. Corralling her hair into a voluminous French twist, putting on her favorite diamond earrings, and carefully lining her eyes while dabbing the dark circles with concealer, Luz transformed herself before Michelle's eyes. In her simple midnight-blue chiffon dress sprinkled with sparkling rhinestones, Luz looked like she was wearing the night sky. Slipping on her silver sandals, Luz smoothed a touch of gloss on her lips, grabbed her clutch purse, and took Michelle's arm, and they went to join the others.

CHAPTER 28

When she boarded the limo bus, Luz was surprised by how many people were in the group. Sacha Bernard had saved a seat for her beside him, next to the window. Before sitting down, she glanced over the group and saw Jeff giving her a look she'd never seen before—a cross between a sheepish smile and loving admiration. He was sitting next to Sara Slattery. Michelle and Clint were smiling and whispering to one another across the aisle. Paul Angel and Christi Cole were grinning too, and so were Mark Miller and his girlfriend. A few other team owners were also on board, including some who'd signed the protest against Roger Schneider. Luz had not remembered that such a big group was going to that night's dinner. Realizing she was the last one to board, she took her seat and visited with Sacha for the short ride to the celebration.

As the little bus wound its way to the destination, Luz

looked around and saw that they were going back to Chateau La Mer. This route on Highway 37 was the one that avoided the mountains: it went through the valley's flatlands to Napa, and then up Highway 29 to the winery. Just thinking about the route through the mountains on the Oakville Grade road made her shudder.

"How much easier it would have been to drive this way! Why didn't I do that?" Luz thought. "Oh, but it was filled with traffic going to the race. Bowman would surely have caught up with us, and Paul and I would both be dead."

This realization hit Luz as they approached the driveway and made their way by the small creek toward the parking lot. She started to feel cold and clammy, and began to panic. Seeing the small duck pond, where tables were set up for cocktails, where the group would enjoy appetizers and champagne, Luz felt anxious, thinking back on her ordeal in the winery's cellar. She didn't want to get off the bus, but she knew she had to.

Her seatmate, seeing the glow of perspiration breaking out along her forehead and temple, and watching her clench and unclench her hands as tears formed in her eyes, stood up when the bus stopped. He announced, "Welcome to Chateau La Mer! Please move from the bus to the patio, enjoy some champagne and light appetizers, and then we shall have a lovely dinner afterward to celebrate."

Luz turned toward the window, shutting her eyes and taking a deep breath or two. Sacha walked down the short stairs of the bus, offered the ladies his hand, and helped the guests find their way to the patio.

Once everyone but Luz was off the bus, Sacha boarded and

sat back down facing her. He handed her his monogrammed linen handkerchief and gently rested his hand on her purse that was in her lap.

"After the war, there were many times I had to enter the cellars at the Chateau Bernard in France. These were the same cellars where my father and I hid many people who would have been prisoners and doomed to death had we not saved them. It is where Orval lived for many years, and Paul Angel too. I remember giving Orval a tour of the Chateau Bernard cellars after we were partners in this new joint venture of Chateau La Mer, and the first couple of times his body would reveal his fear just like yours is doing now," Sacha said tenderly.

"He was a very brave man, just like you are a very brave woman, Luz. Do not be embarrassed or limited by your body's response to an experience that frightened you. Remember that experience is in the past, and it is over now, and you lived through it and saved another's life. You can learn from it, but you do not need to relive it every time you visit the winery or enter the caves. Let it go." Sacha made a vanishing motion with his hand, as if he were a magician making a rabbit disappear.

Luz opened her purse and found a small mirror. She dabbed at the corners of her eyes with the handkerchief that bore the initials *SB*, then touched up her lipstick and dusted her face with powder. She smiled at Sacha, offering him his handkerchief back. "Please keep it, Luz, so you will always remember how brave and clever you are. I hope you carry it with you always."

She closed her clutch and said in a strained voice, "Let's join the party."

Sacha rose from his seat, descended from the luxurious coach, and offered Luz his hand to assist her as she walked down the stairs. Then he offered his arm, beckoned a waiter to bring them each a glass of champagne, and slowly walked her toward a table near the duck pond.

"Luz, much has happened in the last few days since you arrived in the wine country. Not only did you figure out who killed Orval Slattery, but you also kept Chateau La Mer in the hands of the original owners by coaching Sara and me as to what Fred Bowman and Girard Morel had planned. You saved the life of my longtime friend and partner, Paul Angel, and for that I will be forever grateful."

Luz listened intently while she watched the ducks circumnavigate the pond, the female and the drake followed by their ducklings awkwardly paddling after them. For a moment she thought about gentle Orval, who was so kind and generous with his money and his time, sharing his famous wine to benefit charities all over the world. And she thought about how he had died at one of those events, all because of two greedy men, and others who sought vengeance, money and power.

It did not surprise Luz that they were mixed up with Roger Schneider, who was willing to intentionally sabotage several race cars, putting talented people in danger so that he and his team and driver could impress the very man who was talking with her now.

"Sacha," Luz said, "Paul saved me. He shared his water with me. He had the plan to escape. I just followed his lead, then drove the car back to the track with his directions. I am lucky to be alive. Bowman would have killed me if Paul had not been there."

"Ah, Luz, you are a wise woman who shares the credit for her success with others, but never forget it is your thought process that led to that success. Now I should let you join the others, but first I must tell you that tomorrow Christi, Mark, Jeff, and several others from the race team will be flying with me to France so that Christi and Mark can test in a Formula International car. I believe Christi has the talent to be successful there, and it would be exciting to bring the first woman driver into that racing community. Michelle and Clint know of this too, and it has their blessings. I hope you will be happy for everyone if this dream of mine comes true." Sacha sounded content and hopeful.

Luz nodded her head, realizing that Jeff would be leaving with Christi the next day and tonight was their last time to be together for a while. Now she understood Jeff's toast, "Our Formula International chance." It was everyone's dream in racing to make the big show on the international stage, and here was the opportunity, earned by the entire team. She had to be happy for everyone, even though a part of her felt extreme sadness, as if her family was breaking apart. It was time to live in the moment. This evening might be the last time everyone would be together celebrating a race win and at the same time looking forward to a bright future. The Sonoma race signaled the end of the Indy season and possibly the end for Amberson-Harwood's time in this league.

Luz hugged Sacha and gave him a soft kiss on each cheek, then stepped back and said in a wistful tone, "Thank you, for everything." Then she raised her champagne glass to him and brightened her voice. "*A votre santé!*"

Sacha gave her his most flirtatious grin and raised his glass to hers. Their glasses chimed, and both of them swallowed the light bubbles remaining in their flutes. Luz set hers down on the table and turned toward the many people nearby, who were admiring the sunset.

Calmly she walked among the guests, shaking hands, sipping from another glass of champagne handed to her by the same waiter who'd taken care of her and Sacha earlier. Luz made small talk with both of the drivers, congratulating Christi on her big win and her new chance. Mark Miller told Luz that he was looking forward to going on the trip eager to show he had what FIR was looking for in a driver, too. Aimlessly she sauntered from one person to the next, visiting with one team owner about the protest process and how long it would take, and then talking to another to share her thoughts on the entire sabotage event—all the while thinking about Jeff.

On her third glass of fizz, Luz realized she was getting a little tipsy. She hadn't eaten lunch, after all, and she was feeling a bit depressed about the future. She decided to find the seating chart and carefully walk to her place card and sit down. The last thing she wanted to do was fall in the pond on her way to dinner.

Luz focused on the table location and on finding some appetizers to nibble on, since her headache from earlier was returning. She didn't notice that Jeff was right behind her, practically chasing her to the table. It wasn't until she stopped to pick up a plate of cheese straws at one of the cocktail tables that Jeff ran right into her. She'd already popped one of the spicy crackers into her mouth, so when she turned to see who'd run into her, she could only mumble, "Mrf Chs Mrf."

Chewing hungrily, she stared at him and pointed, first at her mouth and then toward the table, and started walking in that direction while motioning for him to follow her. Once she reached the table, she took a big drink of water, patted her mouth dry, and said, as casually as she could, "What's up?" Then she picked up another cheese straw, broke it in half, and ate one and then the other.

Jeff watched her carefully. "Are you OK?"

"Sure, just hungry. No lunch. Too much champagne. I need to eat, but this is all I could find." Luz smiled sheepishly, then ate another cracker and followed it up with more water.

"Oh, yeah. Oh, my god—I guess you haven't eaten for a day or two." Jeff suddenly realized that just the night before, Luz had been a prisoner in the cellars of the very winery where they were about to eat dinner.

"I had a protein bar in the car during the chase through the mountains. I guess that was about ten hours ago. And some water. And a lot of champagne," Luz said. "Anyway, I heard you're going to France tomorrow, and that explained your toast. Very exciting!"

Jeff looked confused.

"The toast you made in my room—'Our Formula International chance.' I hope it goes well. Sacha told me you and Christi were going, and then Mark said he was going too. Nice." Luz could tell she was starting to slip into sadness that she was missing the trip, and had to fight it.

"Yeah, it all came together really fast," Jeff said. "After Christi won and Mark came in third, Sacha brought it up with Clint and Michelle, and they agreed it was a super opportunity."

Luz nodded, now on her fourth cheese straw. She swallowed and said, "Sure, if she can make it, wow, what a great story!"

"Apparently Sacha proposed a joint venture with our team, so if it goes as planned we'll all be part of that circus, but I don't know how it will roll out." Jeff sounded a bit distracted, unsure how Luz was taking his good news.

"I hope it goes well," Luz said. "When's dinner going to start? I'm starving."

Just then the soft gong calling everyone to the tables sounded. Luz looked around the patio, which was lit with fairy lights in the trees, candles in glistening hurricane lamps, and sparkling crystal and silver on the tables. Wreaths of white gardenias encircled the lamps, perfuming the night with a sweet buttery scent.

Sacha Bernard welcomed the crowd with a toast, then introduced Michelle, who congratulated Christi and Mark and she invited Sara Slattery to say a few words.

Beaming, Sara began. "For my first race weekend, it was a doozy. I met all of the winemakers in the valley in my new role as one of the owners of this beautiful place, Chateau La Mer. I was in the pit box with the winning team that overcame all kinds of adversity. And I can't extend enough thanks to Luz Dane for saving the life of our esteemed winemaker, Paul Angel, and for figuring out who murdered my grandfather."

Raising her glass, she continued: "I want to toast the founders, my late grandfather Orval, and my adopted uncles, Sacha

Bernard, and Paul Angel, who are also my partners in this venture, and of course Luz, for without them I would not be part of this wonderful enterprise. *A votre santé!*"

Everyone in the crowd stood, raised their glasses, and repeated the toast. Paul Angel yelled, "Bravo! Bravo!" Sacha whistled and clapped too, while everyone else applauded. Luz smiled at her tablemates as they raised their glasses to her.

After Sara, Michelle spoke up, congratulating the team for their spectacular win that afternoon. In addition, she shared her excitement about the FIR test that both Christi and Mark were going to participate in over the next week. She praised Jeff and all the team members, reminding them that if the two drivers made it to the FIR series, then everyone would be going with them to that exciting racing series. She finished up with a toast, "*Bon Appetit*"

Each course of the dinner was paired with a special wine from Chateau La Mer and other well-known vineyards in the region. Luz was seated with a few of the other team owners and a couple of her teammates. Jeff was at another table, as were Clint and Michelle, Sara, and Sacha. When the small jazz trio started to play for dessert and after-dinner drinks, Jeff asked Luz to dance.

The two of them slowly moved around the dance floor. Jeff talked as they danced. "Tomorrow I leave for Paris. So tonight's the last time I'll get to see you until I get back."

"Yeah, I know." Luz sounded as flat as she felt. She was weary but agitated, and worked hard to keep her emotions in check.

"It's been a rough couple of days," Jeff said softly.

"Yeah, it has." Again she struggled to sound calm.

"Could we have a drink after dinner? At the bar at the hotel? There are some things I want to talk about," Jeff said, nuzzling her neck as he spun her slowly around the floor. The combo was playing a slow samba.

Luz, still tired and a little woozy from the wine, let her head rest on his shoulder. "Sure. After all this."

When the music stopped, they heard an announcement: the bus would be making its first trip back to the hotel for anyone who was ready to return. Luz nodded at Jeff, and grabbed her bag. Then she found Sacha, thanked him for the wonderful evening, and gave him a continental kiss on each cheek to say goodbye. In return he kissed her hand and said, "*Au revoir.*"

CHAPTER 29

Luz took Jeff's arm as they sauntered to the hotel bar, where flames flickered in the small stone fireplace in a corner. Taking a seat on the leather loveseat opposite the fireplace, Luz and Jeff ordered cognac and shortbread cookies.

For a while Jeff talked about the terms of the FIR test and the steps they would have to go through to get ready for the following year's season, which would begin in six short months. He was clearly excited and prattled on about what great publicity they would get in Europe and all over the world. Luz knew what racing in that series would mean: Jeff would be traveling all over the world meeting exotic grid girls and reporters. By the time he was finished with the first season, Luz felt sure she would seem boring and ordinary compared to the women and places he would soon encounter.

Still feeling the fatigue from her last few days, Luz yawned. "So exciting for you, Jeff. It will be good to hear all your stories about the test when you get back home. But right now I'm really dragging, and I think it's time for me to get some shut-eye."

Caught up in his own reverie, Jeff was startled by what he saw as an abrupt interruption of his discussion of the professional challenges he would face in just a day or two. He was so startled that he actually felt offended by her lack of interest.

As Luz stood up, she picked up her clutch, looked for her key, and asked, "Are you going to walk me to my room, or are you staying here?"

"But I'm not finished," Jeff complained. "I need your thoughts on a few of these business issues."

"Oh—business issues. My thoughts. Hmm. Well, if that's what you need, then maybe tomorrow before you leave would be better for us to talk," Luz said. "I'm afraid I might not give you good advice, tired as I am now. My neck is still sore, and that headache is coming back. So we should wait till tomorrow, I think. What time do you have to be at the airport?"

Jeff was annoyed with Luz and could not put his finger on why. He'd been doing all this work, and she'd been away from him, and now when he was getting his big break, she was choosing not to make herself available to him. What was going on?

"Why are you being so difficult? I just have a few questions. I have to be at the airport at eight tomorrow morning, and there won't be time to talk beforehand. So now is the only time I have," Jeff said in a plaintive, faintly cross tone.

Tired and a bit worse for the alcohol, lack of food, and lack of sleep, Luz snapped at him. "It is always about you, isn't it

Jeff? You always need to bounce ideas off of me. You're the one who feels neglected. You're the one who is so insecure that you are jealous of me talking to any man over the age of ten years old. Please, don't think for a minute about how I might be feeling right about now."

"What do you mean? Everyone praised you at dinner. Talked about what a hero you are, how you saved Paul Angel's life, how you saved the winery, how you figured out who murdered Orval Slattery. Tonight was all about you, on a night when the emphasis should have been about the team, about how we won the championship! About Christi and Mark getting the chance of a lifetime to drive in Formula International!" Jeff said bitterly.

At this point the two were nose to nose, and though they were talking in hushed tones, the bartender hustled over to them. "Is there something wrong? Can I get you something else?"

"No!" Jeff and Luz barked at him in unison, then Luz added, in a softer voice, "Just the check, please. I'll be putting it on my room. Number 402. Thank you."

As the bartender moved swiftly to the register to prepare the bill, Luz stood with her arms crossed, tapping her foot and looking Jeff over from top to bottom. Yes, he looked good to her—handsome, strong, with an intelligent face and sparkling green eyes, and a new confidence she had not seen in him before. Maybe she was being shortsighted, and even short-tempered, with all that had happened in the last week. Maybe it was time to make up with him, especially since he was about to leave for Europe and would be away for a few weeks.

As she was signing the check, adding the tip, and folding the copy of the receipt into her purse, Jeff looked her over as well. She was thinner than she'd been even just a week ago, and her concealer barely covered the purple circles under her eyes. A few scabs were visible on her arms and face, probably from her escape from the winery. Yet her features had softness, a more feminine cast, that was not put there by cosmetics; instead it seemed to reflect her growth. When she looked up at him as if to signal that she was ready to leave the bar, he offered her his hand, and they strolled to the lobby and caught the first elevator to her floor.

CHAPTER 30

Her key already in hand, Luz opened the door to her room. Pushing it open, she reached for Jeff's hand and pulled him in, then locked the door behind them.

As they had walked to the room, Luz had thought about Jeff and what he'd meant to her life: how, because of him, she'd become more independent, believed in herself more, and felt more empowered. She now felt like she could live life on her terms. With her own business and her own clients, she could flesh out the other parts of her life as the future unfolded. She thought she could have it all.

Realizing this might be the last time they would be together, for a few weeks or maybe forever, Luz decided that what she really wanted was to spend one more night with Jeff—one more wonderful night.

She wanted to enjoy passionate, loving, tired-from-a-long-day sex and finish with long, slow early-morning-wakeup sex.

This might be her last chance, and she was going to get what she wanted this one last time, making it a night she would never forget. She wanted to run the show, to be in charge for once. Never before had she thought about what she would get from a man—it had always been about what she would give to a man. This was a new way of thinking for Luz, one that held the door open for new possibilities in her relationships. She still wanted true love or at least a love that was true to her, and she to him, but she wasn't sure if that really existed anymore.

When she turned around after locking the door, Luz wrapped her arms around Jeff and pulled him to her, covering his lips with hers and slowly running her tongue over his teeth as she kissed him deeply. When she released him from her kiss, she began to gently cover him with tiny kisses, starting on his chin, then moving down and around his neck to his ears. Gently bending his head toward her, she licked the edges of his ears until he shivered. At this point she could feel him hardening against her, and she carefully taunted him with a feathery touch of her hand. He moaned and threw back his head, exposing his neck to her continued kisses.

She untied his tie and tossed it on a nearby chair, then began to unbutton his shirt, caressing each additional patch of his chest with a small kiss as it was revealed. When she reached his waistline, Luz loosened the clasp of the belt of his pants, unbuttoned the waistband, unzipped the fly, and like two dancers doing the tango, she slowly walked Jeff over to the bed and bent him down on the soft mattress.

Not wanting it to be over yet, Luz stepped back from him, where he could see all of her. She slipped her dress over her head, and her shoes off her feet, revealing her smooth caramel skin and voluptuous curves.

She straddled his thighs, first one and then the other, slipping his boots off. Slowly she pulled his pants off, one leg at a time. Then she turned around to face him and carefully slipped his shirt off, rubbing against him as she removed it. Staring into her eyes as if he was under a spell, Jeff slid his boxer shorts off. With his hands on the sides of her waist, he followed the softness of her hips down to her thighs, caressing her with his fingertips. His touch made her shiver with pleasure.

Jeff beckoned her onto the bed, where her bronzed skin glowed against the white sheets and her dark ringlets spread across the pillow. Gazing at her face, he touched her lips, kissed her eyelashes, and nuzzled her earlobes.

She grabbed his upper arms, where it was white from his truck-driver tan, and with a quick movement rolled the two of them over so that she was on top of him. With a steady rhythm, Luz rode him gently at first but gradually increased her pace that left the two of them shuddering from their shoulders to their toes.

She bent down to give him a full, square kiss on the lips, then collapsed on top of him. In a minute or two she rolled off the bed and picked up the odds and ends of clothes, piling them on one of the chairs. Running the hot water, she prepared a warm washcloth to bathe him, with a hand towel to finish. Touched by this tender ministration, Jeff reached for Luz, but she playfully skipped away.

Luz tended to her own needs, then slid into bed next to

Jeff, who had drifted off to sleep. She luxuriated in the fine percale sheets, and, grateful to be alive and safe, fell asleep with a smile on her face.

CHAPTER 31

Maybe it was the sex, or maybe it was the karate chop and body blows that got her into the storage room at Chateau La Mer, but Luz awoke at around five-thirty feeling sore and sluggish.

Beside her Jeff snored softly, a comforting sound that she missed when they were apart. Looking at the clock on the side table, she saw it was a little before six. He had to be at the airport by seven-thirty, so Luz followed through on her wish list of sleepy-early-morning-sex and slipped under the covers to find him.

"You sure know how to wake a man up in the morning, Miss Dane!" Jeff said. Luz laughed joyfully.

Now it was his turn to rock her in his arms, their bodies moving together as he looked into her eyes. After they climaxed, they held each other tight. Tears flowed down Luz's cheeks, and both of them were overcome with emotion.

"I love you, Jeff."

"I love you too." Luz closed her eyes, memorizing the feeling of Jeff in her arms: his smell, his voice, how his body felt next to hers—everything about him, everything about this moment.

As the light came through the sheer curtains, Jeff asked abruptly, "What time is it?"

"Probably around six-thirty, maybe six forty-five," Luz said. "Check the clock. I can't see it from here."

Jeff looked over and confirmed the time. "I have to go. Still have to finish packing, go to the track, and get to the airport."

"I know, not much time left," Luz said wistfully.

Jeff hugged her to him. "Would you do me a favor? Follow me to the track and then take me to the airport?"

Luz snuggled into his chest, memorizing his scent. "I'll miss you."

"I won't be gone long. Who'da thought I'd be flying to Paris to do a FIR test?"

She opened her eyes and found she was staring into his. "*I* did, for one. I kind of hoped I'd be going with you, but that's not how the cards are playing out this time. I believe you can do anything you want to, Jeff. Anything at all. And be successful at it."

"Why can't you go with me?" He looked puzzled.

"Because I was not invited. And there are only so many seats on the plane." She turned so her back was to him and they were spooned together, then added, "This is a big deal. Sacha is a legend in his land, and you guys are going to slay these people. I know it. Just be you."

Slowly she sat up and slipped out of bed. As she did so, she turned to look at him, grabbed his hand, squeezed it. "I am so proud of you and all you've accomplished this year. This is a big chance for the team and for you. Make the most of it."

Standing up, she beckoned to him to follow her to the bathroom. "Let's take a shower. Time's a-wastin'."

Wanting her memory of this day to be as close to perfection as she could manage, Luz opened her heart to all she could receive from Jeff, and to all she could give back to him, in their few moments alone. Believing this might be their last time together as lovers, Luz refused to feel petulant and frustrated. Instead she concentrated on being caring and loving.

In the past a separation might have meant an argument or a disagreement, so she could feel OK about not being with someone she loved. But this time, learning from her past, she wanted both of them to have a lasting, positive feeling about the two of them together.

Soaping up in the shower gave them another chance to caress each other and enjoy that skin-to-skin contact the slippery bubbles enhanced. Luz lovingly scrubbed Jeff's back, and he returned the favor. After rinsing off, they dried off and got dressed.

"I'm going to run to my room to change clothes and get my bags. I'll meet you downstairs." Jeff pulled on his tux pants and donned his shirt. He added, "I think I might be a bit overdressed for my flight."

Braiding her hair, Luz responded, "You never can tell—those luxury jets can host any kind of party—but yeah, you'd be more comfortable in something else, I think. See you downstairs. "

Luz dressed quickly, selecting a pair of skinny jeans and a long flowered tunic in lavender and periwinkle that accented her blue eyes. She grabbed her purse and scooted down the stairs, arriving just as Jeff got out of the elevator with his rolling bag.

"Great! You're all ready to go. One of the guys can return my rental car, and that way we'll have time to talk on the way to the airport," Jeff said.

Luz nodded. "Sure, that would be perfect." She planned to leave that afternoon after she met with Sara to wrap up any loose ends related to the estate of Orval Slattery. Clint and Michelle were giving her a ride home in their jet, so she had free time this morning. Following Jeff to the track, Luz enjoyed the cool air caressing her curls and face as she drove the little BMW through the countryside. When she drove into the garage area, the team was loading the last few items into the semi.

One of the sanctioning body stewards came up to Jeff and Luz holding a sheaf of documents. He had a serious look on his face.

"Your protest has been accepted by the stewards. Roger Schneider denies any wrongdoing. We've documented and catalogued all of the evidence you shared with us to be used in the hearing. That hearing will take place sometime this fall, before the new season begins. You and the other team owners who were part of this protest will be notified by certified letter at least thirty days before that date," he stated, handing Jeff the stack of papers. "You can represent yourselves or you can hire an attorney."

Luz nodded. "How does the hearing work?"

"There are three stewards who serve on the panel that will hear the evidence and testimony from both sides, followed by final arguments. After that they will rule on your protest allegations, and they'll make their decision known at the end of the hearing. If you don't agree with the decision, you can appeal it to another panel to see if you can get a better outcome," the steward said.

"It sounds like you don't think we have much of a case," Luz said.

"No, I don't have an opinion. I just know that it really depends on how many friends you've got on the panel that hears the evidence. And timing matters too. If they need more teams entering the series, they aren't going to kick someone out before the season starts."

"So maybe it's not worth following through on all this?" she asked.

"No, you want to tell your story, especially because you have other teams involved. Even if they don't find in your favor, people will know what happened, so it is worth it to go through the motions anyway," the chief steward said.

"Thanks for getting this to us so quickly and explaining how it works," Jeff said, shaking hands with the chief steward, then he handed the papers to Luz. "Would you take this back to the shop and put them on my desk in the office? I'll deal with it when I get back from the test."

Luz took the papers, slid them into her purse, and shook hands with the official. "Thank you. What you've shared will help us figure out how to approach this case when the time comes."

The chief steward said goodbye and added, "Have a good break! And Jeff, good luck with the FIR test. We all want to have an American team represented in that series, even if it means we'll be missing you here.

CHAPTER 32

After loading up the car, Jeff and Luz made their way to the private jet center at the Sonoma County Airport in Santa Rosa. On arriving they announced themselves via the intercom at the runway gate. Once they were admitted, Luz drove onto the runway toward the G550 jet emblazoned with the Chateau La Mer livery. A flight attendant with a manifest checked Jeff's name off the list and instructed the ground crew to place his luggage in the cargo hold.

At the bottom of the plane's stairs, Jeff embraced Luz and gave her a long kiss. She looked into his eyes. "I love you! I know this is your dream, having a FIR team, so give it your best shot. I'll be thinking of you every day while you're away."

"I love you too," he said. He kissed her again.

As they broke apart from their embrace, the flight attendant interrupted them by tapping on Jeff's shoulder and saying, "It is time to board, sir. We are already late as it is."

"Jeff, come on! It's time to go," yelled a familiar voice. Jeff and Luz looked up and saw Sacha at the top of the stairs, waving his arms. As Jeff turned to climb the stairs, he and Luz held hands until they were too far apart to continue. At the top he turned around and blew her a kiss before he entered the plane.

Just as she was turning toward her car, Luz saw someone return to the doorway at the top of the stairs. Thinking it might be Jeff, she stopped, only to see Giselle Mouton in a denim mini-dress, thigh to thigh with Jeff, caressing his hair and kissing him full on the lips. Luz felt like a voyeur as she watched the two of them. Seeing Luz, Giselle quickly grabbed Jeff by the shoulders and pushed him further into the shadows of the interior of the plane. In a second Giselle returned and smirked, waving at Luz and blowing her a kiss as the door to the plane closed.

Luz stood tall as she walked to her car, eager to leave as soon as possible, not wanting her emotions to get the best of her. Yes, she felt her heart was breaking, and yes, she wanted to be on that plane. But that was not how things had worked out.

While she was driving slowly away, observing the suggested speed limit for cars on the airport runway, Luz recalled a conversation she'd once had with Michelle and Clint one night over margaritas. They shared with her that their relationship was tempestuous in the first few years, simply because they still had life goals of their own they wanted to accomplish before they each settled down.

Clint wanted to get a handle on understanding the oil

business and to learn about sponsorship in auto racing. When Clint and Michelle first met, she was Miss Winston, and that role obligated her to travel to every track where there was a race. It also required her to kiss every winner. Jealousy was a constant companion for each of them during those years, convincing one or the other that their love had been lost, or that it would never last.

"I knew when I met her that Michelle was a pretty filly, and smart to boot, and there would be men constantly trying to flirt with her or take her away from me," Clint had said.

Michelle added, "And Clint was successful and charmed most of the women who came around, with his country gentleman way."

"It wasn't until one day when Michelle had to leave for a two-week promotional tour with the Cup champion going along with her that I finally gave in and gave up," Clint said. "At that point I realized I had to trust our love and affection for each other and believe that if we were meant to be together, she would come back to me."

"And I did! Even more in love with him than before," Michelle said. "That Cup champion was so stuck on himself, and so self-centered, I was miserable having to be around him all the time. The longer I was away from Clint, the more my love and admiration grew."

"And we've been married twenty-five years this year," Clint announced, patting Michelle's thigh. "I'm not saying it's been easy, but we've both worked on this marriage and worked on ourselves."

"Yes, a marriage is like a garden. You've got to water and

feed it and nurture it, and do your damndest to keep the weeds out of it," Michelle added.

"People will flatter you or flirt with you, even when they know you are married, simply to get what they want, without a care how it will affect your life," Clint said, taking another sip of his margarita. Michelle nodded.

"And it doesn't matter how old you are," Michelle said. "Some people just want what other people have, and then once they have it, they don't want it anymore."

"So if you find that man who makes you feel special, who's smart and who has your best interests at heart and treats you like he cares about you as much as he cares about himself," Clint had told her that day, "then don't give up unless he says he doesn't want you anymore."

At that moment Luz drove through the gate, leaving the runway area. Then she pulled over to the side of the parking lot, her vision blurry from tears. Her body shook as she sobbed, feeling the loss of Jeff leaving her behind as he moved forward to accomplish his dreams and goals.

Where did she fit into all this? Was she just a woman who worked with him and handled the paperwork to make things easier for him, or was she more important to him than that? He'd said he loved her. But did he say that just because she'd said it first, or did he mean it?

And this trip: Giselle Mouton and Christi Cole on the same transcontinental-then-transatlantic flight. They would be together for hours. They'd probably all be members of the mile-high club before they even got to Paris.

Giselle would cover the test for the French magazine she

worked for, the one that was so popular with the billionaire set she catered to in her social media posts. Christi was starry-eyed around Jeff, and now without anyone to intervene, she'd convince him she couldn't succeed without him.

Drying her eyes and blowing her nose, Luz took a few deep breaths to calm down and sipped on the water she'd tossed in the car before they left for the airport.

"What am I doing?" she said aloud, "Trying to make myself crazy? I have a lot to offer any man, so why am I crying over someone I love like he is the last man on earth? Either he'll have the sense to come back to me filled with love or he won't, and that is not about me, it's about him. So I'm going to live my life and do what I want, and I'll see how things play out, but I am *not* going to be weepy and sad and miserable if he doesn't choose me!"

Hearing the roar of the engines of the G550 as it taxied down the runway in preparation for takeoff, Luz looked at her reflection in the visor mirror, patted on a little concealer, and applied a shiny rose lip gloss. She smiled at herself before saying, "That's much better."

Luz looked at the plane at the end of the runway, hearing its engines spool up for the takeoff, then felt her phone vibrate and saw that it was Jeff. Surprised, she answered the phone with a big smile on her face but her voice as casual as she could keep it. "Hey! Sounds like you're about to take off."

"Yeah, I just wanted to talk to you one more time before we were in the air. I want you to know I love you and I'll be back soon. Bye for now." The call disconnected, she saw the big plane rise into the air, and he was gone.

BARBIE O'CONNOR

Thank you for buying this book!

If you enjoyed it, please tell your friends.
Please post a review on Amazon, GoodReads, and other sites.

Read all of the Racing Resort Ranch series.

Virgin at the Speedway
Virgin at Sonoma

Next in the Series:
Virgin at the Racing Resort Ranch

ACKNOWLEDGMENTS

I am so grateful to my friends from the San Antonio Public Library Foundation literary discussion group, *Literary Excursions*, led by Coleen Grissom Ph.D., for their thoughtful analysis of so many books, characters, themes, and ideas. Their insights inspire me as I create my characters and the world they live in.

Especially, I'd like to thank my pre-readers: Anne Church, Susan Cox, Lisa Halff, Mary Henrich, Catherine Roberts, Sandy Ragan, and Mary Rogers, for their concise and valuable criticism of my draft manuscript. Eli Miller of Eli Miller Design guided me through the cover design, helping to create the mystery, energy and dynamism of the combined world of wine making and auto racing in two dimensions. Christi Stanforth, my editor, brought her careful eye to the editing of this book, for which I am most grateful.

In addition, I want to thank Jeff Sakowitz and Dave Smith, driving instructors at the McLaren Performance Driving

School at Sonoma Raceway for their incredible instruction, infinite patience, and valuable experience in the racing field.

As for learning about wine and wine making, I wish to thank Dr. Richard Sclafani who introduced me to the world of wine through a course offered by Lovett College at Rice University. Visiting various wineries in Sonoma and Napa provided an update to my knowledge of the California wine country.

Many thanks to my husband, Toby, for his support, patience, and understanding as I bring my characters and their stories to life in my books. As always, thank you for the ride of my life.

ABOUT THE AUTHOR

Virgin at Sonoma, the second in the Racing Resort Ranch series by Barbie O'Connor, captures the excitement, romance, and energy of motor racing with a mystery twist. Her first novel, *Virgin at the Speedway,* sprang from her experience fielding a team at the 1995 and 1996 Indy 500 races. A fan of all types of auto racing (Formula 1, IndyCar, Nascar, Enduro racing, Drag racing, and Karting), she is also a financial consultant who is the author of the non-fiction book *MoneySmarts4U: The Basics,* intended to help anyone learn the money essentials necessary for success in their adult lives. Barbie O'Connor lives in Texas with her husband and her rescue Havanese-poodle puppy. Please visit her at www.barbieoconnor.com.